Human Trafficking
A Global Perspective

Bright Mills

Ukiyoto Publishing

All global publishing rights are held by

Ukiyoto Publishing

Published in 2023

Content Copyright © Bright Mills

ISBN 9789360164843

All rights reserved.

No part of this publication may be reproduced, transmitted, or stored in a retrieval system, in any form by any means, electronic, mechanical, photocopying, recording or otherwise, without the prior permission of the publisher.

The moral rights of the author have been asserted.

This is a work of fiction. Names, characters, businesses, places, events, locales, and incidents are either the products of the author's imagination or used in a fictitious manner. Any resemblance to actual persons, living or dead, or actual events is purely coincidental.

This book is sold subject to the condition that it shall not by way of trade or otherwise, be lent, resold, hired out or otherwise circulated, without the publisher's prior consent, in any form of binding or cover other than that in which it is published.

www.ukiyoto.com

Dedication

A very special thanks and acknowledgement to the United Nations Organizations, United Nations Office on Drugs and Crime, International Labour Organization, INTERPOL, UNICEF, World Health Organization, and the Department of States for Trafficking in Person United States of America, for their expertise and assistance throughout all aspects of my research and for their help in writing the manuscript.

About the Book

This book is about the illicit crime of Human Trafficking, from a global perspective. The traffickers are making about 150 billion U.S. dollars anually, making it the second criminal organization in the world, after drug trafficking. According to the International Labour Organization, over 40 million people living in slavery worldwide. About 71% of modern day slaves are women, while 25% are children. As per the 2017 Global Estimates of modern slavery released by the International Labour Organisation (ILO) and the Walk Free Foundation (WFF) on Tuesday, an estimated 40.3 million people were victims of slavery worldwide. Women accounted for 71% (29 million), while children constituted 25% (10 million) of modern slaves. Of the 40.3 million trapped in slavery, 25 million were in forced labour and 15 million in forced marriage. Of the 25 million, 16 million were exploited by the private sector, 4.8 million were in forced sexual exploitation, and 4.1 million were in forced labour imposed by state authorities.

Contents

Human Trafficking	1
The Trafficking Scheme	4
Types Of Exploitation	6
Legal Response	8
Human Trafficking As Organized Crime	10
Prevention And Control Of Human Trafficking	11
Facts About Human Trafficking	12
Modern Slavery And Child Labour	18
Trafficked Victims	21
Efforts To End Human Trafficking	23
Health Rights And Services For Trafficked People	28
Italian Outreach Workers	31
The Trafficking Slavery	34
Surviving Stories	37
About the Author	*82*

Human Trafficking

According to the United Nations, Human Trafficking is the recruitment, transportation, transfer, harbouring or receipt of people through force, fraud or deception, with the aim of exploiting them for profit. Men, women and children of all ages and from all backgrounds can become victims of this crime, which occurs in every region of the world. The traffickers often use violence or fraudulent employment agencies and fake promises of education and job opportunities to trick and coerce their victims. The crime of human trafficking consists of three core elements: the act, the means, the purpose. Physical and sexual abuse, blackmail, emotional manipulation, and the removal of official documents are used by traffickers to control their victims. Exploitation can take place in a victim's home country, during migration or in a foreign country. Human trafficking has many forms. These include exploitation in the sex, entertainment and hospitality industries, and as domestic workers or in forced marriages. Victims are forced to work in factories, on construction sites or in the agricultural sector without pay or with an inadequate salary, living in fear of violence and often in inhumane conditions. Some victims are tricked or coerced into having their organs removed. Children are forced to serve as soldiers or to commit crimes for the benefit of the criminals.

According to the International Labour Organization, over 40 million people living in slavery worldwide. About 71% of modern day slaves are women, while 25% are children. As per the 2017 Global Estimates of modern slavery released by the International Labour Organisation (ILO) and the Walk Free Foundation (WFF) on Tuesday, an estimated 40.3 million people were victims of slavery worldwide. Women accounted for 71% (29 million), while children constituted 25% (10 million) of modern slaves. Of the 40.3 million trapped in slavery, 25 million were in forced labour and 15 million in forced marriage. Of the 25 million, 16 million were exploited by the private sector, 4.8 million were in forced sexual exploitation, and 4.1 million were in forced labour imposed by state authorities.

Debt bondage was responsible for 50% of all forced labour in the private sector. This proportion rose to 70% for adults forced to work in agriculture, domestic work, or manufacturing. More women (9.2 million, or 57.6%) than men (6.8 million, or 42.4%) were affected by privately imposed forced labour. The largest share of adults who were in forced labour were domestic workers (24%), followed by the construction sector (18%), manufacturing (15%), and agriculture and fishing (11%). Women represented 99% of the victims of forced labour in the commercial sex industry, and 84% of the victims of forced marriages. As per the Global Slavery Index 2016, India had the world's largest number of modern slaves, at 18.3 million, with 1.4% of the population living in slavery-like conditions.

Also, 151.6 million children aged 5 to 17 were engaged in child labour in 2016. Nearly 50% (72.5 million) were involved in hazardous work. While 70.9% of child labour was concentrated in agriculture, 11.9% worked in industry. The highest number (72.1 million) was in Africa, followed by Asia and the Pacific (62 million). Modern slavery was most prevalent in Africa (7.6 per 1,000 people), followed by Asia and the Pacific (6.1 per 1,000) and then Europe and Central Asia (3.9 per 1,000). Forced labour was most prevalent in Asia and the Pacific (4 per 1,000 people), followed by Europe and Central Asia (3.6 per 1,000), and then Africa (2.8 per 1,000). The latest figures are expected to aid in policy-making aimed at achieving Target 8.7 of the Sustainable Development Goals (SDGs), which calls for effective measures to end forced labour, modern slavery, human trafficking, and child labour in all its forms.

"The world won't be in a position to achieve the SDGs unless we dramatically increase our efforts to fight these scourges. The new global estimates can help shape and develop interventions to prevent both forced labour and child labour," said Guy Ryder, ILO Director-General. According to the ILO-WFF report, the term 'modern slavery' covers "a set of specific legal concepts including forced labour, debt bondage, forced marriage, other slavery and slavery-like practices, and human trafficking." Though not defined in law, "essentially, it refers to situations of exploitation that a person cannot refuse or leave because of threats, violence, coercion, deception, and/or abuse of power."

Human trafficking, also called trafficking in persons, form of modern-day slavery involving the illegal transport of individuals by force or deception for the purpose of labour, sexual exploitation, or activities in which others benefit financially. Human trafficking is a global problem affecting people of all ages. It is estimated that approximately 1,000,000 people are trafficked each year globally and that between 20,000 and 50,000 are trafficked into the United States, which is one of the largest destinations for victims of the sex-trafficking trade.

Although human trafficking is recognized as a growing international phenomenon, a uniform definition has yet to be internationally adopted. The United Nations (UN) divides human trafficking into three categories—sex trafficking, labour trafficking, and the removal of organs—and defines human trafficking as the induction by force, fraud, or coercion of a person to engage in the sex trade, or the harbouring, transportation, or obtaining of a person for labour service or organ removal. Though the United States does not acknowledge the removal of organs in its definition, it does recognize sex and labour trafficking and describes human trafficking as the purposeful transportation of an individual for exploitation.

The Trafficking Scheme

Human traffickers often create transnational routes for transporting migrants who are driven by unfavorable living conditions to seek the services of a smuggler. Human trafficking usually starts in origin countries—namely, Southeast Asia, eastern Europe, and sub-Saharan Africa—where recruiters seek migrants through various mediums such as the Internet, employment agencies, the media, and local contacts. Middlemen who recruit from within the origin country commonly share the cultural background of those migrating. Migrants view the services of a smuggler as an opportunity to move from impoverished conditions in their home countries to more stable, developed environments.

Because such circumstances make it difficult for victims to obtain legitimate travel documents, smugglers supply migrants with fraudulent passports or visas and advise them to avoid detection by border-control agents. Transporters, in turn, sustain the migration process through various modes of transportation: land, air, and sea. Although victims often leave their destination country voluntarily, the majority are unaware that they are being recruited for a trafficking scheme. Some may be kidnapped or coerced, but many are bribed by false job opportunities, passports, or visas. Transporters involved in trafficking victims from the origin country are compensated only after they have taken migrants to the responsible party in the destination country. Immigration documents, whether legitimate or fraudulent, are seized by the traffickers. After this, victims are often subjected to physical and sexual abuse, and many are forced into labour or the sex trade in order to pay off their migratory debts.

The cause of human trafficking stems from adverse circumstances in origin countries, including religious persecution, political dissension, lack of employment opportunities, poverty, wars, and natural disasters. Another causal factor is globalization, which has catapulted developing countries into the world's market, increasing the standard of living and contributing to the overall growth of the global economy. Unfortunately, globalization is a double-edged sword in that it has shaped the world's market for the transportation of illegal migrants, affording criminal organizations the ability to expand their networks and create transnational routes that facilitate the transporting of migrants. The U.S. Department of State adds that the HIV/AIDS epidemic has generated a large number of orphans and child-headed households, especially in sub-Saharan Africa, a situation that creates fertile soil for trafficking and servitude.

Types Of Exploitation

The most prevalent form of human trafficking that results in servitude is the recruitment and transport of people into the international sex industry. Sex slavery involves males and females, both adults and children, and constitutes an estimated 58 percent of all trafficking activities. It consists of different types of servitude, including forced prostitution, pornography, child sex rings, and sex-related occupations such as nude dancing and modeling. Forced prostitution is a very old form of enslavement, and recruitment into this lifestyle is often a booming business for purveyors of the sex trade. Victims of sexual slavery are often manipulated into believing that they are being relocated to work in legitimate forms of employment. Those who enter the sex industry as prostitutes are exposed to inhumane and potentially fatal conditions, especially with the prevalence of HIV/AIDS. Additionally, some countries, including India, Nepal, and Ghana, have a form of human trafficking known as ritual (religion-based) slavery, in which young girls are provided as sexual slaves to atone for the sins of family members.

Forced labour has likely been around since shortly after the dawn of humankind, though there are a number of different forms of modern involuntary servitude that can go easily unnoticed by the general public. Debt bondage (also called peonage), is the enslavement of people for unpaid debts and is one of the most common forms of contemporary forced labour. Similarly, contract slavery uses false or deceptive contracts to justify or explain forced slavery. In the United States the majority of nonsex labourers are forced into domestic service, followed by agriculture, sweatshops, and restaurant and hotel work.

Children are often sold or sent to areas with the promise of a better life but instead encounter various forms of exploitation. Domestic servitude places "extra children" (children from excessively large families) into domestic service, often for extended periods of time. Other trafficked children are often forced to work in small-scale cottage industries, manufacturing operations, and the entertainment and sex industry. They are frequently required to work for excessive periods of time, under extremely hazardous working conditions, and for little or no wages. Sometimes they become "street children" and are used for prostitution, theft, begging, or the drug trade. Children are also sometimes trafficked into military service as soldiers and experience armed combat at very young ages.

Another recent and highly controversial occurrence involving human trafficking is the abduction or deception that results in the involuntary removal of bodily organs for transplant. For years there have been reports from China that human organs were harvested from executed prisoners without the consent of family members and sold to transplant recipients in various countries. There have also been reported incidents of the removal and transport of organs by medical and hospital employees. In addition, there have been claims that impoverished people sell organs such as kidneys for cash or collateral. Although there have been some allegations of trafficking of human fetuses for use in the cosmetics and drug industry, these reports have not been substantiated. In recent years the Internet has been used as a medium for the donors and recipients of organ trafficking, whether legal or not.

Legal Response

Although the practice of trafficking humans is not new, concerted efforts specifically to curtail human trafficking did not emerge until the mid-1990s, when public awareness of the issue also emerged. The first step to eradicating this problem was to convince multiple stakeholders that human trafficking was a problem warranting government intervention. As antitrafficking rhetoric gained momentum, efforts to address human trafficking crossed ideological and political lines. Recognizing the inadequacy of then-existing laws, the U.S. Congress passed the first comprehensive federal legislation specifically addressing human trafficking, the Trafficking Victims Protection Act of 2000 (TVPA). The primary goal of the TVPA is to provide protection and assistance to trafficking victims, to encourage international response, and to provide assistance to foreign countries in drafting antitrafficking programs and legislation. The TVPA seeks to successfully combat human trafficking by employing a three-pronged strategy: prosecution, protection, and prevention. Many federal agencies are given the oversight of human trafficking, including the Departments of Justice, Homeland Security, Health and Human Services, and Labor and the U.S. Agency for International Development. The primary U.S. agency charged with monitoring human trafficking is the State Department's Office to Monitor and Combat Trafficking in Persons (also called the trafficking office).

In addition to the U.S., many governmental entities throughout the world are actively engaged in the attempt to stop or at least slow the activity of trafficking in humans. In 2000 the UN established the Protocol to Prevent, Suppress, and Punish Trafficking in Persons, Especially Women and Children, which provided a commonly accepted working definition of human trafficking and called upon countries to promulgate laws to combat the practice, to assist victims, and to promote coordination and cooperation between countries.

The Office of Drugs and Crime is the UN arm that monitors and implements policies concerning human trafficking and is the designer of the Global Program Against Trafficking in Human Beings (GPAT). Another important international agency with responsibility in this area is Interpol, whose aims are to provide assistance to all national criminal justice agencies and to raise awareness of the issue. Other involved global organizations include the International Labour Organization (ILO) and the International Organization for Migration (IOM).

Human Trafficking As Organized Crime

Human trafficking is a highly structured and organized criminal activity. The criminal enterprises need to transport a large number of migrants over a substantial distance, have a well-organized plan to execute the various stages of the crime, and possess a substantial amount of money for such undertakings. Human traffickers have developed a multibillion-dollar industry by exploiting those forced or willing to migrate. For this reason, migrant trafficking is increasingly recognized as a form of organized crime. Trafficking networks may encompass anything from a few loosely associated freelance criminals to large organized criminal groups acting in concert.

Human trafficking is a lucrative criminal activity, touted as the third most profitable business for organized crime, after drugs and the arms trade, at an estimated $32 billion per year. In fact, narcotics trafficking and human trafficking are often intertwined, using the same actors and routes into a country. Migrant trafficking is one of the fastest-growing criminal enterprises. Traffickers resort to other illicit activities to legitimize their proceeds, such as laundering the money obtained not only from trafficking but also from forced labour, sex industries, and the drug trade. To protect their investment, traffickers use terroristic threats as a means of control over their victims and demonstrate power through the threat of deportation, the seizing of travel documentation, or violence against the migrants or their family members remaining in the origin country.

Prevention And Control Of Human Trafficking

Trafficking is a transnational crime that requires international cooperation, and the United States has taken a lead in promoting intercontinental cooperation. The TVPA provides assistance to foreign governments in facilitating the drafting of antitrafficking laws, the strengthening of investigations, and the prosecuting of offenders. Countries of origin, transit, and destination of trafficking victims are encouraged to adopt minimal antitrafficking standards. These minimal standards consist of prohibiting severe forms of trafficking, prescribing sanctions proportionate to the act, and making a concerted effort to combat organized trafficking.

Foreign governments are to make a sustained effort to cooperate with the international community, assist in the prosecution of traffickers, and protect victims of trafficking. If governments fail to meet the minimum standards or fail to make strides to do so, the United States may cease financial assistance beyond humanitarian and trade-related aid. Furthermore, these countries will face opposition from the United States in obtaining support from financial institutions such as the World Bank and the International Monetary Fund. The U.S. Department of State annually reports antitrafficking efforts in the Trafficking in Persons Report on countries considered to have a significant trafficking problem.

Facts About Human Trafficking

Nearly 80% of human trafficking is for sex, and 19% is for labor exploitation. Researchers note that sex trafficking plays a major role in the spread of HIV. There are more human slaves in the world today than ever before in history. There are an estimated 27 million adults and 13 million children around the world who are victims of human trafficking. Human traffickers often use a Sudanese phrase "use a slave to catch slaves," meaning traffickers send "broken-in girls" to recruit younger girls into the sex trade. Sex traffickers often train girls themselves, raping them and teaching them sex acts.

Organ Harvesting Facts

People are often trafficked for their organs. Human trafficking not only involves sex and labor, but people are also trafficked for organ harvesting. Eighty percent of North Koreans who escape into China are women. Nine out of 10 of those women become victims of human trafficking, often for sex. If the women complain, they are deported back to North Korea, where they are thrown into gulags or are executed.

An estimated 30,000 victims of sex trafficking die each year from abuse, disease, torture, and neglect. Eighty percent of those sold into sexual slavery are under 24, and some are as young as six years old. Ludwig "Tarzan" Fainberg, a convicted trafficker, said, "You can buy a woman for $10,000 and make your money back in a week if she is pretty and young. Then everything else is profit." A human trafficker can earn 20 times what he or she paid for a girl. Provided the girl was not physically brutalized to the point of ruining her beauty, the pimp could sell her again for a greater price because he had trained her and broken her spirit, which saves future buyers the hassle. A 2003 study in the Netherlands found that, on average, a single sex slave earned her pimp at least $250,000 a year.

Although human trafficking is often a hidden crime and accurate statistics are difficult to obtain, researchers estimate that more than 80% of trafficking victims are female. Over 50% of human trafficking victims are children. The end of the Cold War has resulted in the growth of regional conflicts and the decline of borders. Many rebel groups turn to human trafficking to fund military actions and garner soldiers. According to a 2009 Washington Times article, the Taliban buys children as young as seven years old to act as suicide bombers. The price for child suicide bombers is between $7,000-$14,000.

Child Soldier Facts

Many children are trafficked to serve in armed conflicts around the world. UNICEF estimates that 300,000 children younger than 18 are currently trafficked to serve in armed conflicts worldwide. More than 30% of all trafficking cases in 2007-2008 involved children being sold into the sex industry. The Western presence in Kosovo, such as NATO troops and civilians, have fueled the rapid growth of sex trafficking and forced prostitution. Amnesty International has reported that NATO soldiers, UN police, and Western aid workers "operated with near impunity in exploiting the victims of the sex traffickers."

Lady Gaga's "Bad Romance" video is about human trafficking. In the video, Gaga is trafficked by a Russian bathhouse into sex slavery. Human trafficking is the only area of transnational crime in which women are significantly represented—as victims, as perpetrators, and as activists fighting this crime. Global warming and severe natural disasters have left millions homeless and impoverished, which has created desperate people easily exploited by human traffickers.

Over 71% of trafficked children show suicidal tendencies.

After sex, the most common form of human trafficking is forced labor. Researchers argue that as the economic crisis deepens, the number of people trafficked for forced labor will increase. Most human trafficking in the United States occurs in New York, California, and Florida. According to United Nations Children's Fund (UNICEF), over the past 30 years, over 30 million children have been sexually exploited through human trafficking.

Child Trafficking Facts

Human traffickers often target young victims via the Internet. Sex traffickers often recruit children because not only are children more unsuspecting and vulnerable than adults, but there is also a high market demand for young victims. Traffickers target victims on the telephone, on the Internet, through friends, at the mall, and in after-school programs. Several countries rank high as source countries for human trafficking, including Belarus, the Republic of Moldova, the Russian Federation, Ukraine, Albania, Bulgaria, Lithuania, Romania, China, Thailand, and Nigeria. Belgium, Germany, Greece, Israel, Italy, Japan, the Netherlands, Thailand, Turkey, and the U.S. are ranked very high as destination countries of trafficked victims. Women are trafficked to the U.S. largely to work in the sex industry (including strip clubs, peep and touch shows, massage parlors that offer sexual services, and prostitution). They are also trafficked to work in sweatshops, domestic servitude, and agricultural work.

Sex traffickers use a variety of ways to "condition" their victims, including subjecting them to starvation, rape, gang rape, physical abuse, beating, confinement, threats of violence toward the victim and victim's family, forced drug use, and shame. Family members will often sell children and other family members into slavery; the younger the victim, the more money the trafficker receives. For example, a 10-year-old named Gita was sold into a brothel by her aunt. The now 22-year-old recalls that when she refused to work, the older girls held her down and stuck a piece of cloth in her mouth so no one would hear her scream as she was raped by a customer. She would later contract HIV. Human trafficking is one of the fastest growing criminal enterprises because it holds relatively low risk with high profit potential. Criminal organizations are increasingly attracted to human trafficking because, unlike drugs, humans can be sold repeatedly. Human trafficking is estimated to surpass the drug trade in less than five years. Journalist Victor Malarek reports that it is primarily men who are driving human trafficking, specifically trafficking for sex. Victims of human trafficking suffer devastating physical and psychological harm. However, due to language barriers, lack of knowledge about available services, and the frequency with which traffickers move victims, human trafficking victims and their perpetrators are difficult to catch. In approximately 54% of human trafficking cases, the recruiter is a stranger, and in 46% of the cases, the recruiters know the victim. Fifty-two percent of human trafficking recruiters are men, 42% are women, and 6% are both men and women.

Africa's AIDS epidemic has increased human trafficking rates for orphaned children. The AIDS epidemic in Africa has left many children orphaned, making them especially vulnerable to human trafficking. The largest human trafficking case in recent U.S. history occurred in Hawaii in 2010. Global Horizons Manpower, Inc., a labor-recruiting company, bought 400 immigrants in 2004 from Thailand to work on farms in Hawaii. They were lured with false promises of high-paying farm work, but instead their passports were taken away and they were held in forced servitude until they were rescued in 2010. According to the U.S. State Department, human trafficking is one of the greatest human rights challenges of this century, both in the United States and around the world. Today, a slave costs about $90 on average worldwide.

Trafficking Profit Facts

Human trafficking earns $100 billion to $150 billion globally. Human trafficking around the globe is estimated to generate a profit of anywhere from $100 billion to $150 billion. Half of these profits are made in industrialized countries. Some human traffickers recruit handicapped young girls, such as those suffering from Down Syndrome, into the sex industry. According to the FBI, a large human-trafficking organization in California in 2008 not only physically threatened and beat girls as young as 12 to work as prostitutes, they also regularly threatened them with witchcraft.

Human trafficking is a global phenomenon that is fueled by poverty and gender discrimination. Human traffickers often work with corrupt government officials to obtain travel documents and seize passports. Women and girls from racial minorities in the U.S. are disproportionately recruited by sex traffickers in the U.S. The Sunday Telegraph in the U.K. reports that hundreds of children as young as six are brought to the U.K. as slaves each year. Japan is considered the largest market for Asian women trafficked for sex. Airports are often used by human traffickers to hold "slave auctions," where women and children are sold into prostitution.

Baby Trafficking Facts

Pregnant women are increasingly targeted for human trafficking. Human traffickers are increasingly trafficking pregnant women for their newborns. Babies are sold on the black market, where the profit is divided between the traffickers, doctors, lawyers, border officials, and others. The mother is usually paid less than what is promised her, citing the cost of travel and creating false documents. A mother might receive as little as a few hundred dollars for her baby. Due to globalization, every continent of the world has been involved in human trafficking, including a country as small as Iceland. Many times, if a sex slave is arrested, she is imprisoned while her trafficker is able to buy his way out of trouble. Today, slaves are cheaper than they have ever been in history. The population explosion has created a great supply of workers, and globalization has created people who are vulnerable and easily enslaved. Human trafficking and smuggling are similar but not interchangeable. Smuggling is transportation based. Trafficking is exploitation based. Human trafficking has been reported in all 50 states, Washington, D.C., and in some U.S. territories.

The Federal Bureau of Investigation (FBI), in the United States of America, estimates that over 100,000 children and young women are trafficked in America today. They range in age from nine to 19, with the average being age 11. Many victims are not just runaways or abandoned, but are from "good" families who are coerced by clever traffickers. Brazil and Thailand are generally considered to have the worst child sex trafficking records. Nearly 7,000 Nepali girls as young as nine years old are sold every year into India's red-light district—or 200,000 in the last decade. Ten thousand children between the ages of six and 14 are in Sri Lanka brothels. Human trafficking victims face physical risks, such as drug and alcohol addiction, contracting STDs, sterility, miscarriages, forced abortions, vaginal and anal trauma, among others. Psychological effects include developing clinical depression, personality and dissociative disorders, suicidal tendencies, Post-Traumatic Stress Syndrome, and Complex Post-Traumatic Stress Syndrome.

Modern Slavery and Child Labour

40 million in modern slavery and 152 million in child labour around the world. New data reveal that the UN's Sustainable Development Goals, particularly Goal Target 8.7, will not be achieved unless efforts to fight modern slavery and child labour are dramatically increased. New research developed jointly by the International Labour Organization (ILO)1 and the Walk Free Foundation2, in partnership with the International Organization for Migration (IOM)3, has revealed the true scale of modern slavery around the world. The data, released during the United Nations General Assembly, shows that more than 40 million people around the world were victims of modern slavery in 2016. The ILO have also released a companion estimate of child labour, which confirms that about 152 million children, aged between 5 and 17, were subject to child labour. The new estimates also show that women and girls are disproportionately affected by modern slavery, accounting almost 29 million, or 71 per cent of the overall total. Women represent 99 per cent of the victims of forced labour in the commercial sex industry and 84 per cent of forced marriages.

The research reveals that among the 40 million victims of modern slavery, about 25 million were in forced labour, and 15 million were in forced marriage. Child labour remains concentrated primarily in agriculture (70.9 per cent). Almost one in five child labourers work in the services sector (17.1 per cent) while 11.9 per cent of child labourers work in industry. Mr Guy Ryder, ILO Director-General, said: "The message the ILO is sending today – together with our partners in Alliance 8.7 – is very clear: the world won't be in a position to achieve the Sustainable Development Goals unless we dramatically increase our efforts to fight these scourges. These new global estimates can help shape and develop interventions to prevent both forced labour and child labour."

Mr Andrew Forrest AO, Chairman and Founder of the Walk Free Foundation said: "The fact that as a society we still have 40 million people in modern slavery, on any given day shames us all. If we consider the results of the last five years, for which we have collected data, 89 million people experienced some form of modern slavery for periods of time ranging from a few days to five years. This speaks to the deep seated discrimination and inequalities in our world today, coupled with a shocking tolerance of exploitation. This has to stop. We all have a role to play in changing this reality – business, government, civil society, every one of us."

About the data

The new global estimates are a collective effort from members of Alliance 8.7, the global partnership to end forced labour, modern slavery, human trafficking and child labour that brings together key partners representing governments, UN organisations, the private sector, workers' and employers' organizations and civil society in order to achieve Sustainable Development Goal Target 8.7.

Modern Slavery

There are an estimated 40 million people trapped in Modern Slavery. Women and girls are disproportionately affected by modern slavery, accounting for almost 29 million, or 71 per cent of the overall total. One in four victims of modern slavery are children, or about 10 million children. Some 37 percent (or 5.7 million) of those forced to marry were children

Forced labour

An estimated 25 million people were in forced labour at any moment in time in 2016. Out of them, 16 million people were in forced labour exploitation in the private sector such as domestic work, construction, agriculture. About 5 million persons were in forced sexual exploitation, and just over four million persons (or 16 per cent of the total) were in forced labour imposed by their state authorities.

Forced marriage

An estimated 15.4 million people were living in a forced marriage at any moment in time in 2016. Of this total, 6.5 million cases had occurred in the past 5 years (2012-2016) and the remainder had taken place prior to this period but continued into it. More than one third of all victims of forced marriage were children at the time of the marriage, and almost all child victims were girls.

Child labour

152 million children – 64 million girls and 88 million boys – are subject to child labour and account for almost one in ten children around the world. The highest number of children aged 5 to 17 engaged in child labour were to be found in Africa (72.1 million), followed by Asia and the Pacific (62 million), the Americas (10.7 million), Europe and Central Asia (5.5 million) and the Arab States (1.2 million). Approximately one third of children aged 5 to 14 engaged in child labour are outside the education system. 38 per cent of children in hazardous work aged 5 to 14 and almost two-thirds of those aged 15-17 work more than 43 hours per week.

Trafficked Victims

In the past decade, human trafficking has emerged as one of the fastest-growing criminal activities in the world. This modern-day form of slavery claims an estimated 24.9 million victims of all ages around the world and is a serious violation of human rights. Although some trafficking is global, human trafficking is largely a regional and local issue with 65% of trafficking happening domestically. Traffickers use violence, debt bondage, and other forms of coercion to manipulate victims into engaging in commercial sex acts, labor services, or other forms of exploitation against their will. Traffickers particularly target marginalized or vulnerable populations, including children, undocumented migrants, and LGBTQ+ people. Though awareness and concern around this industry have grown in recent years, human trafficking is consistently underreported due to its covert nature, low community awareness, lack of law enforcement, limited resources for victim recovery, and social blaming of victims.

Sex Trafficking

Sex trafficking is the recruitment, harboring, transportation, or soliciting of a person for commercial sex acts through force or other forms of coercion. As a growing global industry, sex trafficking occurs in a wide variety of venues including residential brothels, online escort services, fraudulent massage businesses, strip clubs, and on the streets. Under federal law, any minor under the age of 18 who has engaged in commercial sex is a victim of sex trafficking regardless of whether or not the trafficker used force, fraud, or coercion. The U.N. Office on Drugs and Crime reports that 50% of human trafficking victims were trafficked for sexual exploitation globally. Labor Trafficking Similar to sex trafficking, labor-trafficked victims are coerced; however, instead of being sexually exploited, victims are abused in a variety of labor settings including farms, factories, and domestic work in homes. Trafficked victims in these industries often work long hours and receive little to no pay, but are forced to work by traffickers through debt bondage, violence, or other forms of coercion. Globally, 38% of all human trafficking victims were trafficked for forced labor, and the majority of trafficked men and boys are victims of labor trafficking. Human Trafficking Disproportionately

Affects Women

Though human trafficking affects people across different backgrounds and in all areas of the world, women and girls are disproportionately impacted. Women and girls account for 71% of trafficking victims globally, and the majority are trafficked for sexual exploitation 77% of trafficked women and 72% of trafficked girls are victims of sex trafficking. Resulting from a global tendency to de value women, women who face social and legal discrimination, poverty, or other marginalization become more vulnerable to trafficking. Human Trafficking in the United States Contrary to popular belief, human trafficking also occurs in the United States across all 50 states and Washington, D.C. The U.S. National Human Trafficking Hotline estimates there are hundreds of thousands of human trafficking victims in the United States. In 2019 alone, the National Human Trafficking Hotline fielded 11,500 cases of human trafficking in the U.S. involving over 22,000 victims and survivors. The National Human Trafficking Resource Center found that 41% of sex trafficking cases and 20% of labor trafficking cases reported in the United States from 2007 to 2012 identified U.S. citizens as victims. Of sex trafficking cases reported in the U.S. in that same period, 85% of victims were women. In North America generally, sex trafficking is the most common form of human trafficking, with 72% of all victims on the continent being trafficked for sexual exploitation.

Efforts To End Human Trafficking

The main federal legislation in the United States used to combat trafficking is the Trafficking Victims Protection Act (TVPA), recently reauthorized and amended by the 115th Congress in 2019. The TVPA includes invaluable specialist services for survivors of human trafficking, grants prosecutors new tools to go after traffickers for exploiting others, and enhances partnerships with priority countries to protect children and prevent child trafficking. Additionally, the Justice for Victims of Human Trafficking Act, a bill aimed to end the demand for illegal trade and support survivors, was signed into law in 2015. The federal government has also worked to end human trafficking through the Department of Homeland Security's Blue Campaign, which strives to bring those who exploit human lives to justice. Even with these federal efforts, much work is still left to be done at the state level. All states should have statutes in place that address protection of victims, prosecution, and prevention. Protection must include provisions that cover safe harbor, victim assistance, civil remedies, the ability to vacate convictions for survivors, and strict hotline posting requirements.

Understanding and addressing violence against women

Human trafficking has received increasing global attention over the past decade. Initially, trafficking of women and girls for forced sex work and, to a lesser extent, domestic servitude, were the sole focus of advocacy and assistance. Today, there is recognition that women, children and men are trafficked into many different forms of labour, and for sexual exploitation. Labour-related trafficking occurs in a wide range of sectors, such as agriculture, fishing, manufacturing, mining, forestry, construction, domestic servitude, cleaning and hospitality services. Trafficked people may also be forced to work as beggars or soldiers, and women and children can be made to serve as 'wives'. The most widely accepted definition of human trafficking is found in the United Nations Protocol to Prevent, Suppress and Punish Trafficking in Persons. However, definitions of trafficking vary in practice within and among sectors involved with policy, service entitlements, criminal justice and research.

WHAT IS HUMAN TRAFFICKING

The most widely cited definition of human trafficking is in the United Nations Protocol to Prevent, Suppress and Punish Trafficking in Persons. The recruitment, transportation, transfer, harbouring or receipt of persons, by means of the threat or use of force or other forms of coercion, of abduction, of fraud, of deception, of the abuse of power or of a position of vulnerability or of the giving or receiving of payments or benefits to achieve the consent of a person having control over another person, for the purpose of exploitation.'

How common is human trafficking

Precise figures at the global or even local level remain elusive. Reliable data on trafficking are difficult to obtain owing to its illegal, often invisible, nature; the range and severity of trafficking activities; and variations in how trafficking is defined. These and other factors also blur the distinction between trafficked persons, extremely vulnerable migrants and exploited labourers. Individuals may be trafficked within their own country or across international borders. Trafficking is reported to involve nearly every part of the world as places of origin/recruitment, transit or destination – and this illegal trade in humans is believed to reap enormous profits for trafficking agents. Although women, men and children may all be trafficked for various purposes, trafficking is often a 'gendered' crime. Current evidence strongly suggests that those who are trafficked into the sex industry and as domestic servants are more likely to be women and children. Reports on trafficking of males indicate that men and boys are more commonly trafficked for various other forms of labour, and that these trafficking sectors generally differ by country or region.

What do we know about the health effects of human trafficking

To date, evidence on health and human trafficking is extremely limited. A systematic review published in 2012 identified 16 studies, all of which focused on the violence and health problems experienced by trafficked women and girls. Most studies focused on trafficking for forced sex work and only two included data on trafficking for labour exploitation. The health-service needs of victims and survivors have received woefully limited attention particularly when compared with law-enforcement and immigration responses to trafficking. Because research on health and trafficking has been conducted almost exclusively on sexual exploitation, evidence generally focuses on sexual health (especially related to HIV) and, to a lesser degree, mental health. Knowledge about the health risks and consequences among people trafficked for non-sexual purposes remains scarce.

Many trafficking studies rely on data from case-records from services providing care to repatriated sex-trafficked girls and women. Data have been collected on, for example, HIV status or other sexually transmitted infections (STIs) and health conditions such as tuberculosis. There have also been a small number of studies conducted with women who were still in sex work settings, but the application of varying criteria on who was 'trafficked' means it is difficult to draw reliable conclusions. For people who are trafficked, health influences are often cumulative, making it necessary to take account of each stage of the trafficking process. At each stage, women, men and children may encounter psychological, physical and/or sexual abuse; forced or coerced use of drugs or alcohol; social restrictions and emotional manipulation; economic exploitation, inescapable debts; and legal insecurities. Risks often persist even after a person is released from the trafficking situation, and only a small proportion of people reach post-trafficking services or receive any financial or other compensation.

Sex trafficking and health

To date, few prospective studies have been done on the health needs of trafficking survivors. A 2006 quantitative study in Europe documented the physical, sexual and mental health symptoms experienced by women trafficked for sexual exploitation. In this multi-site survey of approximately 200 women, the majority reported high levels of physical or sexual abuse before (59%) and during (95%) their exploitation, and multiple concurrent physical and mental health problems immediately after their trafficking experience. The most commonly reported physical health symptoms included fatigue, headaches, sexual and reproductive health problems (e.g. STIs), back pain and significant weight loss. Follow-up interviews with the women revealed that mental health symptoms persisted longer than most of the physical health problems. Similar results emerged from research using physician-administered diagnostic interviews in the Republic of Moldova, which found prevalent, persistent and comorbid psychological symptoms in women in post-trafficking services. A survey in Nepal also confirmed the preponderance of mental health problems in women trafficked for forced sex work .

Labour trafficking and health

It is important to recognize that women, men and children are trafficked into many forms of labour and vulnerable to a range of occupational health risks, which vary by sector. The risks can include poor ventilation and sanitation; extended hours; repetitive-motion activities; poor training in use of heavy or high-risk equipment; chemical hazards; lack of protective equipment; heat or cold extremes; and airborne and bacterial contaminants. Exposure to such risk factors can result in exhaustion, dehydration, repetitive-motion syndromes, heat stroke or stress, hypothermia, frostbite, accidental injuries, respiratory problems and skin infections. Health and other effects associated with trafficking overall

• Poor mental health is a dominant and persistent adverse health effect associated with human trafficking. Psychological consequences include depression; post-traumatic stress disorder and other anxiety disorders; thoughts of suicide; and somatic conditions including disabling physical pain or dysfunction.

• Forced or coerced use of drugs and alcohol is frequent in sex trafficking. Drugs and alcohol may be used as a means to control individuals and increase profits, or as a coping method or by the trafficked person as a coping method.

• Imposed social isolation, such as prevention of family contact or restriction of a person's movements, is used to maintain power over people in trafficking situations, as is emotional manipulation by the use of threats and false promises.

• Economic exploitation is widespread. Trafficked people rarely have decision making power over what they earn and may be charged by traffickers for 'services' or 'supplies' such as housing, clothes, food or transport. These usurious practices often lead to 'debt bondage'.

• Legal insecurities are common for people who travel across borders, particularly when traffickers or employers confiscate identity documents or give false information about rights, including access to health services. This may not only limit people's use of medical services but also lead to unjust deportation or imprisonment. Trafficked people may not be acknowledged as victims of crime but instead treated as violators of migration, labour or prostitution laws and held in detention centres or imprisoned as illegal immigrants.

• Trafficked people who return home may go back to the same difficulties they left but with new health problems and other challenges, such as stigma. For those who try to remain in the location to which they were trafficked, many encounter the insecurities and stresses found in asylum-seeking and refugee populations. People who manage to leave a trafficking situation, whether they return to their country of origin or not, are at a notable risk of being trafficked again.

Health Rights and Services For Trafficked People

Article 6, subsection (3) of the United Nations Protocol to Prevent, Suppress and Punish Trafficking in Persons encourages, but does not require, signatory states to provide medical assistance for trafficked persons (Box 2) (1,2). No guidance is offered on the type of health services that should be made available or when, and under which circumstances, such provision should be made.

GOVERNMENT OBLIGATIONS TO THE HEALTH OF TRAFFICKED PEOPLE

According to the United Nations Protocol to Prevent, Suppress and Punish Trafficking in Persons: 'Each State Party shall consider implementing measures to provide for the physical, psychological and social recovery of victims of trafficking in persons ... in particular, the provision of: (a) Medical, psychological and material assistance'. The health sector has an instrumental role to play in the prevention of trafficking, and care and referral of trafficked people. Sexual health outreach workers and practitioners assisting migrant populations are well placed to address trafficking. For example, health workers may have opportunities to alert individuals to the risk of human trafficking; identify and refer people who are in exploitative circumstances; and provide care as part of a post-trafficking referral system. Reports suggest, however, that a great deal of awareness-raising and sensitization is required to enable health and service practitioners to provide safe and appropriate care in human trafficking cases. Key barriers include language and cultural differences; inadequate information; limited resources; poor involvement of victims in the decision-making process; lack of training and knowledge on human trafficking and care; and issues of stigma, discrimination, safety and security.

Best Approaches to deal with Human Trafficking for Policy Makers

At a policy level, regulatory steps are needed to increase awareness of the risks of human trafficking, especially among individuals intending to migrate. Migrant workers in destination settings should have the same protections and legal redress mechanisms as those in the domestic workforce. Recent positive developments include the 2011 adoption of the Convention on Domestic Workers, which includes special measures to protect vulnerable members of this employment group, and the Dhaka Principles, a guide for companies on responsible recruitment and employment of migrant workers. Governments should mandate acute and longer-term provision of health care to trafficked persons. This could be achieved, for example, by granting such individuals immediate rights to state-supported health services, regardless of their ability to pay or willingness to participate in a criminal action against traffickers, and committing the necessary financial and human resources.

For Health Care Providers

Health care providers and organizations involved with trafficked persons should increase their capacity to identify and refer people in trafficking situations and provide sensitive and safe services to people post-trafficking. Examples of support for health practitioners working with trafficked people include Caring for trafficked persons: guidance for health providers, a guide by the International Organization for Migration and the London School of Hygiene and Tropical Medicine and Human trafficking – key messages for primary care practitioners, an online resource provided by the Health Protection Agency in England.

For Researchers and Funders

Empirical research on human trafficking is limited. Particularly lacking are studies on larger, more potentially representative samples of trafficked people, and longer-term studies to better understand post-trafficking health changes. Empirical data on trafficking of men, their health needs and service access, is especially scarce. Similarly, more data are needed on trafficking across the full range of labour sectors involved. Rigorous evaluation studies of policies and programmes are needed to identify the most effective counter-trafficking strategies and most appropriate care for the people affected.

About the Alliance 8.7

Alliance 8.7 is a global strategic partnership committed to achieving Sustainable Development Goal Target 8.7 , which calls on the world to "take immediate and effective measures to eradicate forced labour, end modern slavery and human trafficking and secure the prohibition and elimination of the worst forms of child labour, including recruitment and use of child soldiers, and by 2025 end child labour in all its forms". Alliance 8.7 seeks to achieve Target 8.7 and related Targets 5.2, 16.2, 16.3 and 16.a through the alignment of global, regional and national efforts, and by focusing on accelerating timelines, sharing knowledge, driving innovation and leveraging resources.

Italian Outreach Workers

According to the Italian outreach workers, there has been a significant shift in the migration pattern from Africa with many more young Nigerian women coming. And they add that many, if not most, of the young Nigerians arriving on Italian shores know they will be expected to engage in sex work. But the women have little idea how harsh their living conditions will be and how long it will take for them to pay off the debts they owe the traffickers who recruited them and got them to Italy. Few of them break free from the work, according to Appiah, a 37-year-old Ghanaian migrant. "I know of four women in the last few years," he says forlornly. "Two of them had been working for years and managed to pay back what they owed the traffickers; the other two were young and fled to Germany." For the last few years Appiah has been working for an Italian charity in Castel Volturno, a decaying seaside town north of Naples that's become home to thousands of his fellow countrymen and migrant women from Nigeria. Another charity in the area says that since 2010 about one hundred Nigerian women have sought its help to break free from sex work. Italian and European authorities estimate as many as 16,000 Nigerian women, some as young as 16 or 17-years-old, have been trafficked into Italy in the past two years by Nigerian racketeers and crime gangs, the most notorious a syndicate known as Black Axe.

The number of unaccompanied Nigerian women sailing to Italy from Libya has risen each year from 1,454 in 2014 to more than 11,000 last year and the International Organization for Migration estimates as many as 80 percent of them work once they arrive as street prostitutes for traffickers often in brutal conditions and for little pay. Like the Italian authorities, IOM argues the Nigerian women are forced unwillingly into prostitution, tricked by traffickers, who charge the women as much as 35,000 euros for the trip to Europe. The traffickers terrify the women into submission, using violence, voodoo religious rites and threats to harm the women's families back in Nigeria, say authorities.

Threat of violence

But the picture is more complicated, according to charity workers and migrants themselves, who suspect most of the Nigerian women who've arrived in the past two years — and the ones setting out now to complete a highly dangerous journey through strife-torn Niger and Libya — were not tricked by unscrupulous recruiters but knew they'd be engaged in sex work in Italy. They say the women, most in their teens or early twenties, do not understand how harsh their conditions will be and how vulnerable they will be, prey to violence and manipulation in a culture they struggle to understand. Breaking free isn't easy — the voodoo blood oaths traffickers make them take back in Nigeria weigh heavily on many of the women, the threat of violence is ever present and some fear their families will be harmed. "The reality is that some of them, I would say most of them, know they will be involved in prostitution," says Pescara-based Fabio Sorgoni, an official with the Italian charity On the Road, which helps prostitutes get out of sex work. "Some of them think they'll be working in factories or cleaning. But a large proportion of them know they're coming to do sex work," he adds.

Anti-migrant rage

With anti-migrant rage mounting in Italy and populist parties demanding tough action to halt the record influx of asylum-seekers, charity and outreach workers fear to speak too openly about the motives and backgrounds of the Nigerian women arriving in Italy. They do not want to erode what is left of public compassion for asylum-seekers. "The pattern has changed a lot," says Maureen, a Nigerian migrant who arrived in Italy 20 years ago, starting life here as a housemaid. Working her way through school, she is now a case officer for the charity Associazione Jerry Masslo. "A few years ago, yes, the women were duped by the traffickers' and expected ordinary jobs. But those days are over...the position has changed." Partly so, she says, because of the effectiveness of outreach programs in Nigeria warning women of the dangers. She says many of the recently arrived Nigerian women were sex workers before in Nigeria. "Some families, often mothers, sisters, and aunts urge them to make the trip, arguing it'll just be for a few months and then they'll be rich," she explains.

Motivated by poverty

Poverty and the lack of job opportunities in Nigeria led them into sex work in the first place, she argues. "And they don't understand how bad it will be for them in Italy," she says. Says Sorgoni: "The women don't understand 35,000 euros is lot of money. When they get here, they have to stay on the streets for 14 hours a day and they get something like 5 or 10 euros for sex. They then realize they'll have to be on the streets for years — forced to go with everyone, forced to have sex without a condom because many clients here demand that." He adds: "Many are very young; they come from rural areas and are unschooled. They don't understand their own bodies or the infections they can get and they think all they have to do is pray, or ward off sickness with voodoo rites." In Castel Volturno, local doctors say nearly a quarter of the Nigerian women they treat have sexually transmitted diseases. "They fear they'll be arrested when they arrive at the hospital," says Dr. Beniamino Schiavone, director of Clinica Pineta Grande, a cutting-edge private hospital the government subsidies to provide care for migrants in the area. "So they wait until their problem is terribly serious."

The Trafficking Slavery

Most people think that slavery ended with the signing of the Emancipation Proclamation, not so! Human trafficking is a worldwide crime that ruthlessly exploits women and children into forced labor and sex. It is the modern form of slavery and a violation of human rights. It is the fastest growing criminal activity in the world, which generates over $150 billion annually, with >70% of the dollars spent are from the United States.1 The hidden nature of this crime makes it a huge problem today, but one in which no one wants to think about or address. This topic is designed to raise your awareness, enrage you, and inspire you – enraged that human trafficking exists today as the fastest growing and most lucrative crimes, and to inspire you to reach out to help one of the most vulnerable populations trapped in slavery. Human trafficking is a form of modern day slavery in which traffickers use force, fraud, and coercion to control victims for the purpose of engaging victims in commercial sex acts or labor services against his/her will. Sex trafficking has been found in a wide variety of venues within the sex industry, including residential brothels, escort services, fake massage parlors, strip clubs, and street prostitution. Labor trafficking has been found in diverse labor settings including domestic work, small businesses, large farms, and factories.

The International Labor Organization [ILO] estimates that there are 27 million victims of human trafficking globally, with hundreds of thousands in the United States. The victims of this crime in the United States are men, women, children, and foreign nationals. The Asia-Pacific region accounts for the largest number of forced laborers in the world, followed by Africa and Latin America.2 It is hard to combat this problem because victims are often afraid to go to authorities for help. Human trafficking is a market-driven criminal industry that is based on the principles of supply and demand, like drugs or fire arms trafficking. It does not exist solely because many people are vulnerable to exploitation, but instead it is fueled by a demand for cheap labor and for commercial sex. Human trafficking thrives for several reasons: ☐ Low risk – traffickers perceive there to be little risk or deterrence to affect their criminal operations due to lack of government and law enforcement training, low community awareness, ineffective laws, lack of law enforcement investigation, scarce resources for victim recovery, and social blaming of victims.

High profits – When individuals are willing and able to pay for commercial sex and forced labor, they create a market and make it profitable for traffickers to sexually exploit children and adults in the sex trade and labor industry. Traffickers exploit others for the profit they gain from commercial sex and from forced labor. They lure people into forced labor and sex trafficking by manipulating and exploiting their vulnerabilities. The majority of victims are women and girls, though men and boys are also impacted. Traffickers prey on people who are hoping for a better life, lack job skills or opportunities, have unstable home lives, run away children, homelessness, or have a history of sexual or physical abuse.4 Traffickers promise a high paying job, a loving relationship, or new and exciting opportunities and then use physical or psychological violence to control them. Traffickers can be lone individuals or part of an extensive criminal networks, all which have the same mission – exploiting vulnerable people for profit.

Although human trafficking victims are thought to be a problem affecting women, men are also victims; in some parts of the world, they're victimized more often than women. It is estimated that 98% of sex trafficking victims are female and 2% are male.5 Identification may be difficult due to lack of awareness of the part of health care workers and, most victims won't speak up due to shame and humiliation. A misconception of the public is that victims of human trafficking will immediately ask for help and will self-identify as a victim of crime. The reality is that victims of human trafficking often do not seek help or self-identify themselves due to a variety of reasons, such as lack of trust, self-blame, or specific instructions by the traffickers on how to behavior in public. There is frequently a negative consequence for the victim if they reach out to the police or medical personnel. Trust building is often needed to uncover the victim's whole experience. Health care workers need to be able to recognize the potential 'red flags' and indicators of human trafficking and report them so intervention can take place. The following indicators may identify a potential victim of human trafficking:

Is not free to leave or come and go at will

Is unpaid, paid very little or only through tips

Works excessively long and unusual hours

Is fearful, anxious, depressed or tense

Avoids eye contact

Appearance that doesn't match stated age

Is not allowed breaks or unusual restrictions at work

Owes a large debt and is unable to pay it off

Lacks medical care or is denied medical services when needed

Appears malnourished and shows signs of physical abuse

Is not in control of their own money or possessions

Has several inconsistencies in their story when asked

Loss of sense of time

Surviving Stories

"An empowered survivor makes traffickers vulnerable"

Malaika Oringo from Uganda is the founder and CEO of Footprint to Freedom, a survivor-led organization that believes the only way to eradicate human trafficking is by giving survivors a voice and the opportunity to lead. She is also a member of the International Survivors of Trafficking Advisory Council (ISTAC). For the past 17 years, Malaika has been intensively involved in the fight against human trafficking, as a representative of the Salvation Army at the EU Affairs Office in Brussels and more recently as a global consultant on anti-human trafficking efforts. She campaigns for victims' rights and works to strengthen survivor inclusion and engagement in decision-making processes. Malaika has a special interest in her home country Uganda and in the neighbouring countries of Rwanda, Kenya and Tanzania and also in Burundi. Her East Africa Programme supports survivors of human trafficking who have returned home to reclaim their lives and raises awareness of human trafficking among vulnerable communities.

Malaika Oringo

This is her story.

I decided to enter this field because I am passionate about fighting for social justice and standing up for those who cannot speak for themselves. I feel it is my calling. Being a survivor of human trafficking gave me more reason to advocate on behalf of survivors especially after getting my freedom almost 17 years ago. I realized that freedom is more than the moment of exiting from slavery, freedom is rather an ongoing journey and a process which requires continuous support from all stakeholders including survivor leaders. Moreover, I joined this field because I believe my freedom is not worth having if it does not include the freedom of others. I use my experience to promote best practices, to bridge policy gaps and offer services to educate, inspire and empower.

I am not a stereotypical survivor, because I am not defined by my victim's past, but instead I carry my victim's scares as a badge of honour, as an inspiration to other survivors that there is life at the end of the tunnel. I turned a bad experience into something positive. Today, I am using the pain from my past to lead others out of exploitation. I have given my invisible scars a place where it no longer hurts and have turned the pain into wisdom. It's almost 17 years now since my exploitation ended. I can say that there is no ending date for recovery; the healing journey is a process. Nevertheless, mentally, I do not suffer as much. Physically, I am healthier than ever before, spiritually, I still have triggers and bad dreams, but I wake up knowing I am safe. When I was 15, I was living in Kampala and my mother died. I needed support and went to find a family member at a camp for displaced people. A man approached me. It was obvious I was new to the camp and was not sure where to go.

The man was white, a European. He was dressed like an aid worker and carrying a bible. I told him my story, and he said there were people in his country who would help me go to school. I was naïve, I believed him. I had even prayed to God to help me and thought this man was my saviour. I needed to trust someone. He even told me not to tell anyone, because he only had a place for one person and if others knew about this opportunity, they would want to come too. He got me a passport and we went by car to Kenya then flew to Luxembourg. I was very excited. At the airport, he handed me over to two men and two women and I never saw him again. We then went by car to Amsterdam. I realized I had been deceived when the pimp who the trafficker sold me to said that I am 'his property' and I 'owe him a lot of money'. I was exploited for around a year.

I became very sick, and since the traffickers did not take me to hospital, they dumped me on a roadside in winter with no jacket. I was found and placed in a safe house for minors. The support was short-lived. Just like in most countries, the duration of the assistance offered is linked to the ongoing trafficking investigation. When it stopped the support stopped too. This sudden removal of rights, support, and legal discrimination exposed me to re-victimization and gender-based violence. The trafficker was never convicted. I was rushed into the process of victim identification and didn't get enough time to reflect. I was in a shock, I blamed myself and I didn't identify myself as a victim, because I didn't understand what human trafficking was. I had no rights to medical care, accommodation, and schooling for over 10 years. This left me on the verge of being re-trafficked. I faced stigma and loneliness. When I was 18, I had to leave the accommodation for minors and was helped by the church. I started speaking out about my experience and at one event when I was 19, I said that all I wanted was to go school.

I was approached by a Dean of a private university and he offered me a scholarship. I was supported further by some other teachers and the church. Today I have a bachelors and a master's degree. Countries should strengthen support for victims and provide long-term support for survivors there's no quick fix to recovery. A lot of survivors must deal with the aftermaths of their exploitation without sufficient help. My surviving experience also made me realize that survivors are speaking, but they are not being heard. There are gaps in how survivors are positioned in the anti-human trafficking field. Survivors are being re-exploited because to most organizations they're a currency for donations and for marketing. So, survivors are reduced to being just the story and dehumanized in the process. The United Nations should foster survivor engagement and inclusion among its Member States in research, policy, and integration intervention decisions. Most human trafficking legislation is passed without hearing from those people who have actually been impacted by the crime. We can't talk about partnership, collaboration, and policies as fundamental international frameworks to combat human trafficking without including survivor leaders as stakeholders.

I can acknowledge that in recent years, progress has been made to include survivors. But, it's still quite unusual for the voices of survivors to feature significantly in international trafficking debates. Yet survivors' voices are very vital in establishing effective anti-trafficking strategies that address prosecution, protection, and prevention. The survivor's narrative is significant in crafting the right policies and practices because survivors know first-hand how human traffickers operate and which strategies they use to bond victims to slavery. Survivors know about the traffickers' recruitment strategies, their grooming practices, their violent tendencies, their weaknesses, their mentality, the tactics they use to escape the law. Survivors should be at every decision-making table from the community level to national and international levels. They should hold equal powers in making decisions on how to combat trafficking and how to serve and support those victimized by it.

Survivor scholarships should be provided so survivors can have success in careers of their choice. There should be safe housing and trauma-informed services, access to safe employment. Without these, survivors of human trafficking remain vulnerable to the cycle of exploitation. For organizations working directly with survivors, be aware of tokenism inclusion of survivors. Find ways better ways to engage survivors as partners in your organization with paid positions. More needs to be done to address human trafficking as a form of gender-based violence. I fell prey to human trafficking because of the demand for gender-specific exploitation, driven by male exertion of power and control over women and the fascination of sexually exploiting young girls. To date women and girls are being trafficked for: sexual exploitation, forced prostitution, "contractual" marriage to mention a few. These listed purposes of trafficking are typical gender-stereotypes of work and often driven by male desire to control over women, thereby increasing their risk of gender-based violence. My message to victims of human trafficking is this: what words describe who you are beyond the trauma you have experienced?

Focus on finding that person. I believe survivors can heal. It might take some time but there is life at the end of the tunnel and remember you are not defined by your traumatic experience you can rise above it and reclaim your purpose. Be careful in the way you share your story, so that you won't be re-traumatized, and when you are psychologically and emotionally ready to speak up or advocate, I urge you to turn your experience into wisdom. I know, today that if I had not done anything with my trauma, my purpose would have been misguided. Dare to dream, find your purpose, claim it. Survivors are so much more than the trauma they've endured. We can't undermine how badly human trafficking affects victims. I'm proud to be able to be in a position that allows me to create change.

"Recovery is a process. It isn't always easy, but none of us needs to do it alone."

Kyra Doubek, from the USA, is the Executive Director of Washington Trafficking Prevention, (WTP) a survivor-led organization committed to ending human trafficking in Washington State by empowering vulnerable communities. Through their 'Coalitions Against Trafficking', WTP has mobilized local communities to raise awareness and host events. WTP provides comprehensive, survivor-centered prevention and intervention education to schools, families, and community agencies. Kyra has led groundbreaking anti-human trafficking initiatives with federal and local law enforcement authorities, supporting them with the development of anti-trafficking protocols. She campaigns for an increase in services for human trafficking survivors.

Kyra Doubek

This is her story.

Most people only know me as a survivor of domestic sex trafficking, less known is that I have also been exploited for labour. Labour trafficking is not assigned the importance that it deserves. We cannot continue as a society to assign more value to only certain classes of exploitation. Currently, I serve as the Executive Director of Washington Trafficking Prevention (WTP). This role is completely different than any role I've ever held in the past. Previously I worked for the Organization for Prostitution Survivors as an advocate, and later at Kent Youth and Family Services in Washington State as a behavioural health specialist, I remember all the important lessons that I learned from the people I worked alongside. Those experiences inform the partnerships that WTP nurtures, the awareness events that we host, and the programmes that we develop.

While working at Kent Youth and Family Services, I had the opportunity to partner with Kent Police Department to provide advocacy, outreach, and services. While serving in this role, I received referrals daily from law enforcement, community members, service providers, and educators. I saw a recurring pattern of people who were groomed for exploitation online and survivors of human trafficking who had a history of abuse, unmet needs, poverty, and marginalization. Most of these situations are preventable, and there are multiple situations where an intervention can be made. My hope is to create a world that no longer supports or sustains systems of marginalization that make people vulnerable to exploitation. Every time I read a study about the mortality rates of people who experience exploitation, I always feel like I'm one of the lucky ones. Sometimes I feel guilty because I was able to access services and support when I needed them. When I say I'm a survivor, I mean that I am actually still alive and survived it. Many survivors of exploitation die by homicide from a pimp or a buyer.

Even less talked about is death by trauma. Many of us end up leaving the life of exploitation and abuse, but because of the inability to access specialized services, we die from overdose or by suicide. I grew up in a home and a family where cycles of untreated trauma, substance abuse, poverty, domestic violence, and sexual assault were common. Before I turned five, I was sexually assaulted by a family member, and experienced physical abuse and neglect from my primary caregivers. The instability and violence that I grew up with seemed normal. Part of that instability I experienced growing up was a frequent relocation. Moving frequently prevented me from building a support system and friendships. My lack of social support and feelings of isolation made me desperate for any kind of attention I could receive. When I was 12, America Online had become readily available to the public.

Internet chat rooms became the place where I tried to fulfill my need for love and belonging. I lied and said I was 14 years old, and I encountered droves of adult men who were excited to talk to a 14-

year-old girl online. Fast forward a couple of years, and the abuse at home became untenable. When I finally ran away at 14, I experienced multiple assaults, homelessness, domestic violence, and began using substances to feel better. Unfortunately, my substance abuse did not actually solve any problems, and made me easier to manipulate and control. I met my first pimp when I was 16 years old on the internet. We would talk online for hours, and I felt like he really understood me and cared about me. He told me he was going to take care of me and that nobody was ever going to hurt me as long as he was around. When we met everything was fine at first, and he seemed like the perfect guy. The bond that he fostered with me online was calculated and focused. He knew about the kind of home I grew up in, the abuse I experienced, and that I had no support systems. It was easy for him to isolate me from my very small circle of family members. He convinced me to end those relationships or sabotage them, and when he finally had me alone the abuse and exploitation started.

Even though I got the courage to finally leave that relationship, it did not solve my problems. I tried many times to rebuild my life and get a normal job. My trauma always seemed to precede me, and I had difficulty obtaining affordable housing and a stable job that paid a living wage. This resulted in me moving in with abusive boyfriends to stay off the streets. In my mid-twenties, I met my last pimp. At that time, I had a job that didn't pay me enough to survive on my own, and he told me about a website where you can get dates and make easy money. He started marketing me and running my ads. On December 10th 2012, I was on my way to meet a sex buyer and crashed my car into a police vehicle. Luckily the officers were okay, and I was arrested for driving under the influence. Being in jail for 90 days gave me the opportunity to separate myself from the situation that I was embedded in and begin accessing help. Once I began accessing services for addiction and mental health, the impacts of my trauma came to the surface. I had recurrent flashbacks, night terrors, insomnia, memory issues, anxiety when in public settings, depression, and suicidal ideation. The impacts of PTSD were debilitating, and I thought I would never get better. I firmly believed that I was at fault for all of my exploitation. For the first year and a half out of the life,

I had a really hard time focusing, remembering simple tasks, and taking care of normal life tasks.

I was fortunate to reconnect with my friend Judy, who became my mentor. Judy said something that changed my life. "There are three steps to getting over any resentment. Step one: get over it." I remember being flooded with outrage when she said this. She continued: "Step two: stop wishing it hadn't happened. And step three: do something to help somebody else, in a way that only you can help them because you experienced what you experienced." That conversation has been a guiding light to healing from so many aspects of my trauma. Like with so many survivors, my traffickers were never convicted or charged. I was too afraid to pursue charges, and once I was ready the statute of limitations had passed. After a few years, I landed a job at Kent Youth and Family Services working closely with Kent Police Department to serve people who were suspected, confirmed, or at-risk of sexual exploitation. There are many people who praise how far I've come, but truthfully, I still struggle and feel like an imposter in any space I'm in. I haven't recovered from being trafficked, it's a process that will likely be lifelong. Sometimes I still have flashbacks about seemingly innocuous things like songs, smells, body language, phrases, loud noises, or gestures.

Sometimes there's a false belief that because I'm in a leadership role, I'm completely healed and impervious to the impacts of my experiences. There are no "perfect survivors", and it's a harmful falsehood that we need to stop perpetuating. Trauma recovery looks different for everyone, and our stories are all different. That's why there needs to be survivor leaders from every community and background to address the problem. Survivors are instrumental to preventing and ending human trafficking. There are so many ways survivors must be involved, such as serving on a board, running organizations, volunteering, providing direct outreach services, or speaking with elected officials. I encourage the United Nations to continue to listen to survivors and support policy approaches that survivor leaders recommend. To any of my survivor siblings out there, remember healing from our experiences is a process that isn't always easy. Get connected to people who are safe and that you can depend upon for the times when you are struggling. One of the best decisions I made was to connect with other survivors. They normalized all the challenges and barriers I was facing, like experiencing trauma, financial insecurity, loneliness, shame, and guilt. No matter what happens, no matter how imperfect your journey might look, keep trying.

"Being a survivor of trafficking in persons is like having a tattoo on the soul. No one can see it, but it is always there and remains forever."

Marcela Loaiza from Colombia runs the Marcela Loaiza Foundation to raise awareness about human trafficking through education in Colombia and the United States. The Foundation helps victims to reintegrate into society and provides services to overcome personal and psychological problems and gain access to the job market. She currently lives in Las Vegas where she runs a health spa and works as a life coach and has published two books about her experience. In 1999, she was tricked into accepting a job offer in Japan to work as a professional dancer. Instead, upon arrival in Tokyo, her passport was removed and she was forced to work as a prostitute to pay off an alleged debt of 50,000 USD. This ordeal lasted for 18 months.

Marcela Loaiza

This is her story.

I've always felt the need to motivate people spiritually, so they can learn to better manage their emotions, which is why I became a life coach. I love to help people feel proud and accept who they are, and my spa has allowed me to do that. The main purpose of my foundation is to help bring awareness to the general public about human trafficking in order prevent this crime. We also provide financial, legal, and psychological support to victims. The goal is to help victims reintegrate back into society. I give workshops on entrepreneurship to women who have suffered from a psychological trauma. I motivate them to develop their skills, so they can be more productive and pursue their own dreams. I experienced human trafficking in the form of sexual exploitation. It changed my life forever. Thanks to therapy, I was able to move on from those experiences and close that chapter of my life.

I became a true survivor when those negative experiences were no longer ruling my emotions and decisions, and when I was strong enough to turn it all into something positive and use my story to educate others. When I was younger, I wanted to be a professional dancer and travel the world, but I trusted the wrong people and fell into the traps of traffickers. I was 21 at the time. I realized I had been deceived the moment I was forced out onto the streets on the first night I was in Tokyo. My rights were all taken away, and I was treated as property. I knew it was the worst mistake of my life, and that's when the psychological abuse started. I was told that if I managed to escape, I wouldn't make it to my daughter's funeral in time. I was sexually exploited for 18 consecutive months in Japan without a break. I was not rescued, I managed to escape after a client helped me.

As soon as I returned from Japan, I was able to see my daughter and family. After I returned to my country, I was very paranoid and suffered from PTSD. I pressed charges, but nothing was ever done. I never received any support from the state and the case did not hold up in court. This all happened before the law against human trafficking was put in place in Colombia. At first, I did not see myself as a victim. I felt very guilty for many years for trusting my traffickers, so because of this I just kept silent. The judge I pleaded my case to also made me feel guilty for having left Colombia with my traffickers willingly, and he told me he did not believe my story was true. It wasn't until I received psychological help that I realized I was a victim. Even after publishing books about my experiences, there are still a lot of people who believe I am responsible for what happened to me. They don't see me as a victim and try to make me feel responsible. Being a victim of human trafficking changes your life forever. The recovery process is long and painful, and I would say it's always ongoing.

Finishing my psychological therapy was the first step to recovery, publishing my books was the second step. This process of recovery led me to reintegrate back into society, move on with my life and even be happy. However, the scar is always there. It might not be a physical one, but it is a small reminder of what I have endured. The emotional trauma never really goes away, and I strive to not let it affect my life or define me. Every victim is different and not many can get to a point where they help others through their experiences. Everyone goes through different coping mechanisms. The crime might be the same, but the experiences are different, and the healing process is unique to each person. Victims should focus on healing themselves before they can even consider helping others.

I do feel that having survivor testimonies are incredibly important and these stories should be respected accordingly. It's not easy to stand in front of an auditorium and relive your trauma. The people that do so are doing it for the sole purpose of bringing awareness and not because it's easy for them. This job should be compensated with scholarships, trainings, workshops, and have those survivors become human rights ambassadors for the United Nations. I think having celebrities as ambassadors is fine, but the amazing testimonies of a lot of survivors could have an even bigger impact because of their example of resilience. I think we need to give more value to these stories that serve as examples to society. My message to victims would be to not give up. They should not wait around for support from the government but rather take their own rehabilitation into their own hands. They need to learn to love themselves, to believe in themselves, and to better themselves. Knowledge is the best tool anyone can have because it brings about new opportunities that would not have come otherwise.

"I will continue to remind survivors of human trafficking how powerful they are."

Karly Church from Canada is a Crisis Intervention Counsellor at a regional support service for victims of human trafficking. Karly meets with politicians and visits community centres to raise awareness of the crime and speaks openly about her experience as a victim of sexual exploitation. The school board for Durham Region has also approved a presentation given by Karly and her colleagues as part of the curriculum for all grade nine classes. They talk to 13 to 14 year olds about sex, consent and online safety and discuss the warning signs of human trafficking. Karly also teams up with the Anti-Human Trafficking Unit of the regional police force, joining them on operations.

Karly Church

This is her story

I started working with the police about three years ago on a scheme that's centred around bringing survivors of human trafficking together with frontline workers. Any time they meet with a potential victim, I go with them. It's very difficult to engage and support individuals who've been trafficked because often they don't see themselves as a victim or even realise that they're being trafficked. 85 percent of my clients see their trafficker as their 'boyfriend'. Since I started this role, there's been a 93 percent increase in the number of people who want to provide a statement or speak to the police. The police officers arrange a fake date by phone. They go in plain clothes, show their badges and the first thing they say is that the person is not in any trouble, and they have someone outside who is independent from the police – this is me. I go into the room alone. Anything I'm told, I can't tell the police. I make a quick disclosure that I worked in the sex trade and was exploited. When I let them know I have had similar experiences, there is a bit of a relief.

It's very difficult to talk to someone about the sex trade who hasn't been there and doesn't know how difficult it is. Imagine what it's like when policemen enter the room, you might not have any clothes on, you're anxious you may be in trouble, and there's a lot of stigma to working in the sex trade. You feel ashamed. Hearing my story also instils a bit of hope. When you work in the sex trade, when you have been trafficked, it gets to a place where you think this is the best it's going to get. It's lonely. You're often by yourself in hotel rooms and the only company you have is with other sex workers or the people you're having sex with. When someone comes in, is respectful, non-judgmental, and talks to you, there is hope, that maybe there is a way out. The majority of victims say they don't want to leave their situation and deny being trafficked, although all the signs are there. If they do choose to flee, I make sure everything is set up for them. It's fundamentally unfair to ask a victim to leave their trafficker if you are unable to meet all their basic needs. I talk about my story as often as I can. Although I went through something negative, today I get to flip it for a positive. If my story can help one other person, it's not just a heavy negative load that I need to carry around all my life, there's a purpose to it. Not everyone who has been through such an experience would feel the same way, but my healing is through telling my story. My early life shows some of the vulnerabilities that made me more susceptible to trafficking. It shows how quickly it can happen and can happen to anyone.

I came from a very small town, with just 1200 people. It was a seemingly normal family. Two parents, an older brother and sister, a roof over our heads, food on the table. But, like in most families, there were things going on behind the scenes that affected me growing up. There was very little social support in my town. So, I kept things to myself. I learnt from a young age not to ask for help. My dad was away a lot for work. He almost always had two jobs, and I never really saw him. He never came to any school events. So, in my little kid mind I thought he didn't love me. I was child number three, and I would see photos of family camping trips with my older brother and sister, but I never did this. My mom had her own issues and was not really emotionally available. She never asked about my day or came to school events. I was a very sensitive child, very anxious. I thought I was unlovable and missed a lot of school, and began acting out, but no one noticed. I also experienced sexual violence but did not tell anyway. I basically stopped going to school, I just didn't care. At a young age I started using drugs. They became the cure to all my problems, took away all the pain of my past and made me feel normal.

By 15, I was a full-blown drug addict and had to put something in my system every day to survive. It cost a lot of money. I had to do things in order to access those drugs usually from men, and the sexual violence continued. I would exchange sex for drugs or a place to stay. This was my life for around three years. My family didn't see me much at that point, and my parents were going through a separation. No one noticed until finally my older sister realised something was wrong. My family flew me to British Colombia for drug treatment, and I was clean for four months. A week before I finished, I called my dad. He said he was sorry, but the family was not going to fly me home, as they felt the appropriate support was where I was. All I wanted to do was to make my family proud.

I left treatment and within 20 minutes, I found my drug of choice and the cycle began again. Exchanging sex for drugs. My sister then flew me to Toronto. I had never lived there before. I was clean when I arrived but within a couple of weeks, I was using again and got kicked out of the sober living house and was in a women's shelter. I felt hopeless. I kept trying to get better and falling back to square one. I tried again and went to a detox centre but got kicked out with another girl. I remember it was freezing cold. I only had a backpack with one change of clothes. No one would take me in, I had burnt my bridges with my family. I had no cash and no phone.

The girl I got kicked out with said I know a place where they have drugs, and they will take care of us. Drug dealers came and went, and for two days I exchanged sex for my drug of choice. Then these two men came in and they were different from everyone else. One came over to me right away. He saw my vulnerabilities. I was an easy target. He knew I was out of place, in a new city and homeless and had a serious drug addiction. He said what are doing here, you don't belong here. You are so beautiful. No one had been that nice to me in such a long time, so instantly I was hooked. He sat down next to me and asked me a million questions. It felt incredibly special that for once someone noticed me and saw I was struggling. That is where it started, when he started to lure me. He asked about my life, my family, my friends, why I was not in touch with my family. He asked about my hopes and dreams for the future. He was really gathering lots of information that he could use against me in the future, but at that moment it just felt so good that I told him everything. I even told him I had been exposed to sexual violence.

He asked me what had happened to me in my past that causes me to use drugs today. That blew my mind, because it was the question, I had been waiting for someone to ask since I was a little girl. My family and friends had never asked me this, and he had known me just five minutes. I knew he was a drug dealer, but I felt he was treating me like a human being. I thought he was a nice guy and genuine. Obviously, he was looking at my basic needs that were not being met. I had not eaten or showered in days. I had no money, no phone. He took me out of the apartment, got me food and a hotel room with my own key. He gave me a sense of safety and security. He got me my drug of choice, which was a basic need at the time. Next day, he took me shopping and bought me clothes. He boosted my self-esteem and self-worth. He said he would take care of me and not let others hurt me. He introduced me to his friends and gave me that sense of belonging to a family that I really wanted. Withing 48 hours, he had given me everything I was lacking.

At first, he never mentioned the sex trade. He said I would be making lots of money doing drug runs. When he started asking me to do sex work, I thought it was just to pay him back for all he had done to get me on my feet. But he took total control, took photos of me, posted my advert. He decided how many hours I would work, how many people I would sleep with in a day and which services I would provide. He put his number on the advert and at the end of the day, he would take all the money. It was horrific. I hated every minute of it. The majority of the time I did not know who was coming to the door or what services I was expected to provide. He was not around 24/7. Physically I could have left, the room was not locked. But his manipulation was psychological and the trauma bond he created was strong. He was a bit violent but not too much. It was more to instil that fear in me and show me what he was capable of. His control was more psychological. For me the grooming, the luring, the manipulation is much stronger than the physical violence and I think pimps are starting to realise this.

If you get beaten up every day, especially from the beginning, you are going to run. But if you believe you are with someone who loves you, who takes care of you, meets your basic needs and has actually taken you out of a situation that was much worse, well even if you have to do things you really don't want to, you have a bed to sleep in, you are not alone, you get to eat. We moved into three different hotels in three cities. It's quite a blur how long I was trafficked. I was lucky because detectives found me just before I was supposed to go to another province with him where his brother was a trafficker. We would have been on a plane two days later. The police saw my advert online, saw the red flags and booked a fake appointment. I opened the door thinking it was a client, and it was a detective, he was in plain clothes. He showed me his badge and said I am with the police and here to make sure you are safe. It was incredibly lucky. That officer changed my life, I would not be here today if he hadn't done what he did. I did not agree to go with the officer straight away. He checked the room was safe. He asked if he could sit down and have a conversation.

It sounds bizarre, but he did everything that my trafficker did when I first met him. He did not judge me. He did not tell me that what I was doing was wrong. He asked about my life, my family, my friends, my hopes and dreams for the future, my struggles. He started to build the relationship. I denied I was being trafficked and said I was an independent sex worker who kept all my own money. The trafficker had told me what to say. But there were the red flags. I had no money on me, I did not have a phone, I did not know which services had been booked. Then my trafficker called and he said the hour is up and another client was waiting. The officer knew I was being trafficked. He gave me his number on a piece of paper from my items and said I should contact him if I needed anything. He left my room, but the investigation continued. He spoke to the hotel staff, did more digging, found out another room had been booked in the hotel using the same phone. The traffickers were found and arrested.

I was not relieved when I was told this. I was really angry. I was screaming and crying, because they had taken away the only people who were supporting me. After the traffickers had been arrested, the detective came to my hotel room to get me. He said, you have to leave, but don't worry, we will make sure you are somewhere safe. He assigned me a victim service worker who got me a phone, financial support, and a bed at a drug treatment centre. She met my needs and helped me to reconnect with my family and friends. After I finished treatment, she found me a place to live. If I had not had that support immediately, I would have gone back. The cycle would have continued. The two men were charged. One took a plea deal. In the other case it lasted for two years. Both men were not found guilty of human trafficking offences but of lesser charges. I have the trauma of being trafficked and the trauma of having to testify in court. It was equally difficult. To be called a liar, questioned on the stand, face my trafficker, see the photos and videos of myself in court, I was retraumatized.

The detective said to me no matter what the outcome is Karly, guilty or not guilty, this is a win for you and for us. To see where you are today compared to how I found you in that hotel room. That is a win! When I heard that they had not been found guilty of human trafficking, I was devastated. I wanted to return to familiar behaviours, but in my head, I heard "this is still a win for us". I was 24 when I got out of it, now I'm 32. I still have a great support network and still have bad days, but my dad now tells me how proud he is of me. We have built a strong relationship. The detective is still a part of my life too. We speak once or twice a year. I'm now most proud of the awareness raising work I do. People do not want to believe that this is happening in their community, to their children or the friends of their children. They need to understand that this could happen to anyone.

My biggest contribution is sharing my story. I speak to politicians and tell them about my experience and the need for a victim-centred approach. I will not stop telling my story. The most resilient people I have ever met are those who have experienced something similar. They have the ability to bounce back and move mountains. They can change their lives and those of the people around them. I will continue to remind survivors of human trafficking how powerful they are, how much potential they have, and what they can offer the world.

Don't let the exploitation be the end, turn it into something great."

Francisca Awah from Cameroon is the founder and Executive Director of The Survivors' Network. This organization, which is led by survivors of human trafficking, rescues women from national and international situations of exploitation, and empowers them to rebuild their lives and be reintegrated into society. The Network also runs awareness raising campaigns among vulnerable communities in Cameroon, especially in rural areas of the country. Since it was launched in 2015, the Network has supported the rescue of over 2,000 victims of human trafficking. In 2018, Francisca was honoured by the U.S. Department of State for her work against human trafficking.

Francisca Awah

This is her story:

In 2010, I went to Norway to do my master's degree in human rights and multiculturalism. There I became a victim of sexual abuse. In 2012, to escape from this situation, I had to return home to Cameroon before I had even finished my studies. I had such a difficult time. I could not find a job and in 2013 become a mother. Then in 2015, I saw an advert in a newspaper about English teaching jobs in Kuwait. The man who had posted the advert was from my village. I knew him from my childhood. He came to visit me and said how well educated I was and that he had seen how I was struggling since returning from Norway. He mentioned that the salary I was getting at that time was way too little for my level of experience. And my life was tough. I could not take care of myself or my young son. The trafficker had actually studied my vulnerability.

He said he would send me to Kuwait to teach English if I paid him several hundred dollars. I was excited and happy about this possibility, because it was a way to work and take care of my family. This is how he managed to traffic me. He was part of a bigger network. When I got to Kuwait there was no English teaching job. A family met me at the airport and took my passport from me. I never saw it again until I managed to escape three months later. I was forced into domestic servitude and worked long hours with no food or medical attention, and I was in a lot of pain. I was never paid. In three months, I worked in three houses. When I left one house, I would go back to the agency, which is basically like a shopping mall where lots of maids are sitting there waiting for people to buy them. In the last house where I was forced to work, I stayed for two months and two weeks. I kept a diary and wrote about my ordeal every day. The lady of the house was from Lebanon and had three sons. I told her that my mother in Cameroon could no longer look after my son. I had never been paid, so I could not send money to her, and I wanted to return home.

She said, "Francisca , you are like the TV in my room. You are a commodity and need to work. We bought you. If you want to go home, then pay us back and then look for money for your flight." I realised that I needed to escape and even considered selling my kidney to pay for the airfare back to Cameroon. I had seen an advert in a newspaper and contacted a family that wanted to buy a kidney for a lot of money. It was not until the day they were coming to collect me to take me to the hospital that I changed my mind. They kept contacting me, so I had to block their calls. One day when I was working in the kitchen, I saw a TV feature about CNN's Freedom Project and organizations that fight against modern-day slavery. I made a note of the names and since I never had a break, I would go to the rest room and contact the organizations. I got lots of automatic replies, but then an organization in New York, Freedom for All, replied to me and we started to communicate. I also joined a Facebook group with other women from Cameroon. One said she would pick me up so we could run away. Freedom for All guided me through this escape process.

Usually, when the family left the house, they locked the door. But on one Friday, the wife was in Lebanon with two of the sons, and the husband and oldest son were going to pray. The man had been sexually abusing me. I had been pretending that I was enjoying it, so I could gain his trust. It worked, and he left the door open on that fateful Friday. I ran from the house, leaving my clothes behind, and with the other woman from the Facebook group, I got in a taxi. I went to the embassy of the Central Republic of Africa and there I found 17 other maids seeing refugee. They let me in and called my employer, asking him to return my passport. He did, but I was told that if I did not leave Kuwait within a week, the employer would bring charges against me. I had no money to pay my flight, but Freedom for All supported me and in less than four days I had left Kuwait. It was not easy when I returned to Cameroon. I was stigmatized by my family. They said, Francisca has done it again. She went to Norway but struggled to make a good life. Now she was in Kuwait and failed again, nothing good will come of her.

This pushed me to tell my family what had really happened to me and explain what I had been through. Then I started to talk within my community too and tell people that just because you get on an airplane and travel abroad, it does not mean that you are already successful. So, this is how I started my journey, by telling my story. I was contacted by other survivors of human trafficking who had been rescued with the help of Freedom for All, and we formed our network. There is a lot to do. We are a team of 15 volunteers in the Survivors' Network. We rescue women and children from exploitation in Cameroon, and help to repatriate victims from the Middle East, the Gulf States and other parts of Africa. Fifty percent of our work is based on economically empowering the victims once they have been returned home. If this is not done, they can fall victim to being re-trafficked. We need to make sure that rescued women can earn a living, many of them have no qualifications. We provide vocational training, teach women how to write business proposals and launched a micro finance scheme so women can start their own small businesses. Recently, we opened a shelter for rescued women. Many of them have no place they call home, so this is a pace where they can stay and receive counselling. The Network also does a lot of awareness raising work in Cameroon, where a lot of people do not know what human trafficking is, especially in rural areas. We want to prevent women and children from falling prey to traffickers, so we visit communities, schools, churches and markets to conduct workshops.

The majority of the people we speak to really believe what we are saying. Some realise that they have been victims of domestic trafficking or that their children are currently being exploited. My work now is not just a job, it is my life. This is how I got through my ordeal. But it is difficult to heal. There are quiet times when the memories return and you feel really low. The trafficker who tricked me ran away to Europe. He had trafficked over 70 women, including his own girlfriend, and had made a lot of money. My message to other victims of trafficking is that it is never too late to pick up the broken pieces and start over. You don't know where it will lead to. Don't let your situation be the end. Turn it into something great. Organizations like the United Nations should provide a space for survivors of human trafficking. A place where survivors of different backgrounds, cultures and countries can come together to share experiences and discuss what we really need. And when such big organizations are looking for the facts and data, come and see us. See what we are doing. The real information will come from us.

"It is a tremendous injustice to be sold as a child and indebted as an adult."

Kendall Alaimo from the USA is an international anti-human trafficking activist, a clinical educator and a professionally trained artist. She is passionate about child sexual abuse prevention. Kendall campaigns for the development of effective clinical care for victims of human trafficking and better educational opportunities for survivors of this crime. She serves on the International Survivors of Trafficking Advisory Council (ISTAC) of the Organization for Security and Co-operation in Europe (OSCE). ISTAC is made up of 21 survivors of human trafficking from 14 countries who advise the OSCE on anti-trafficking policies.

Kendall Alaimo

This is her story

I lost my childhood to child sex trafficking and a decade of my young adulthood. It is a miracle that I am alive today. What survived is my voice, and I am using it for change. If I can speak to the world on behalf of survivors of modern-day slavery then the message that I want to be heard is that victims of this crime must have access to appropriate health care and academic opportunities. This is based on my own lived experience as a survivor and my expert knowledge of the community of human trafficking survivors. I ended up having trauma care for over a decade. I worked with many physicians from the West to the East coast of the U.S.A. I felt I had lost. But then I changed the narrative to 'have gained'. And what I gained was a very rich knowledge about the lack of clinical care not just in the U.S.A but around the world for people like me – normal people that went through abnormal experiences.

At times, I felt that I was educating the clinicians about my symptoms more than they were actually treating me. My symptoms were science based. We know that with the higher levels of trauma someone goes through, the higher levels of clinical symptomatology and complex pathology they are going to have. These are not 'crazy' people. They are resilient ones. With clinic care for survivors of human trafficking, we must innovate unique approaches for complex post-traumatic stress disorder (PTSD). We have great PTSD care for veterans and military personnel. But we cannot take the medical models that we are applying for veterans and apply them in the same fashion to survivors of modern-day slavery, especially child victims, because their brains are still developing. We need to have dialogues not just about PTSD in survivors but also about another subcategory of conditions known as dissociative disorders. If we do not treat these in survivors of human trafficking, there is a high risk of suicide over their lifetime. We have university programmes in trauma care, but we really do not have enough curricula in child sex abuse, and we certainly do not have enough training on how to apply medical methods to survivors of modern-day slavery.

I am very passionate about speaking to current and future clinicians on how to interact with victims of trafficking. They must have very strong ethical standards, because if they are not practising with good boundaries and good ethics, they can actually retraumatise this population and cause a lifetime of more symptoms. When you are trafficked, whether as a child, for sex or labour exploitation, you become objectified. You are a commodity for others who benefit from you financially or otherwise. So, when you are treating someone who has been objectified, you have to treat them in a human way, because you are treating dehumanization. Treating this population is a privilege. The doctor should not be an authority figure or abuse any power dynamics in treatment. When you are treating a survivor of human trafficking there needs to be an equal playing ground, the work must be ethical, collaborative and safe. There is an International Society of the Study of Trauma and Dissociation, they are doing great work, but we need to do much more.

I know that as a survivor of child trafficking, organized criminal abuse and torture, it takes a very brave and ethical clinician to be witness to these experiences. There are not enough clinicians who are well versed in trauma-informed care, and it can cause a lot of damage. The need for more trained clinicians in this field is desperate. Alongside campaigning for more effective clinical care, I also advocate for better educational opportunities for survivors of human trafficking. I have seen parallels in difficulties with access to healthcare and education, and we need to address this in a policy-based way. Exiting trafficking does not mean that you are free. Being free means getting access to housing, long-term mental health care, education and then economic equity. Healing from all forms of exploitation can be a lifetime journey. Education is an important part of this journey. I often say, 'we must educate to liberate'. We really need to ensure that survivors of human trafficking can get educated in the curriculum they chose, so then they have a chance of landing the career of their choice.

When you are forced to work in an abusive way, work in a sense becomes a trauma. Survivors must be able to obtain a career role they feel safe in performing, so they can maintain employment throughout their lifetime. By creating pathways to academic opportunities, survivors can be integrated into society, become economically independent and ultimately liberated. This also reduces the vulnerability of re-exploitation. But education is not free in many countries, and many survivors cannot afford to go to college. Many, like me, ended up with medical debts from the care they needed because of what they had endured. It is a tremendous injustice to be sold as a child and indebted as an adult. My dream is to become a therapist and fill the gaps that I experienced in clinical care. I want to research dissociative disorders, to provide a needed service to my community of survivors and have the ability to listen to patients as a trained witness. I actually applied to graduate school multiple times, and I have had to turn down acceptances at universities because I could not secure the funding to attend. In 2017, I got awarded a presidential scholarship to a school in Boston but it did not cover all the cost. I got on a bus with my acceptance letter and headed to New York City to meet with New York University to inquire if I could attend that fall. While the Professor I met with supported my mission, they said they could not offer me a way. In 2020, I got accepted into Northwestern University. I lit a candle on my desk every day and prayed I would find a way to attend. I even had a phone meeting with the Executive Office of the President at the White House. People from across the United States were cheering me on, a letter was drafted by the larger community to the institution on my behalf. I sat through the orientation session, but at the last minute I could not find a way to secure my seat in time.

I know I was not entitled to a scholarship but to me attending school was not a luxury but was in fact my social responsibility. I felt a deep responsibility to obtain a piece of paper that would ultimately aid me in saving lives. I know many survivors that also cannot attend university, because they have trafficking-related debts, or they are not residents in the country where they want to study, so they cannot take out federal loans. In some cases, their credit rating has been destroyed because their traffickers had taken out money with their social security numbers. So, like with my journey to get healthcare, I also faced adversity with my own journey to get an education. But I say that solutions are born out of challenges. Now I am working on what will hopefully be a global initiative to create seats at universities for survivors of human trafficking. My hope is that universities will embrace these dialogues, and I look forward to celebrating them as they join us in liberating those in need. As survivors we have a vital role to play in the anti-human trafficking community. Our narratives must not merely be inspiring but the lessons that lay within them must be used to create lasting solutions.

Just like I want to become a clinician, other survivors want to fix and fill the gaps in after care and get justice not just for the crimes that were perpetrated against them but also justice for their peers. These people are the most resilient individuals I have ever encountered. They have overcome slavery, gone through years of clinical care, saved their own lives and now the only thing they desire is to selflessly serve their community by going to school and obtaining professions to help remedy these human rights violations. They want to become doctors, lawyers, and policy makers. Just last week, I got an email from a survivor whose healing journey I know was long and hard. They emailed me to inform me that they had gotten into a prestigious doctoral programme and had just two days left to find a way to attend before they had to turn down the offer. After reading that email, I wept. It validated to me the importance of this education initiative I am now undertaking.

I want to note that lived experience cannot be taught in a classroom and the grit, determination and passion these survivors have cannot be manufactured. If given a chance, I know they are truly capable of changing our world. I am often invited to speak at all kinds of events, conferences and on panels, and while I really appreciate that, I know we need to take it to the next level. We must start with conservations about solutions and meet to discuss the pinpointed ones. Then we should bring in experts from the fields of healthcare and education and actually come up with concrete solutions and put them into policies. Then we have to take these policies and make sure that they are actually implemented and are successful. If they are not, we need to go back and rework the framework and make these policies more effective and hold participating states accountable for their implementation. What does freedom really look like? My favourite part of the day is when I let my dog Winston off his leash by the lake in the morning. It brings me a sense of peace to witness him having the freedom I am still seeking for myself and others. The most powerful question you can ask a survivor of human trafficking is 'do you feel free?'. And they will say yes or no. If they say no, you need to ask, 'what is it going to take for you to feel liberated and how should we work as a community to meet your needs?' The United Nations needs to reach out to survivors in multiple countries and really get a better understanding of what they need. It could be shelter, food, medical care, or education. I think the UN can do this by having dialogues with survivors like me about what these specific needs are, and how can we find the solutions to meet these needs.

The Office is committed to supporting Member States in implementing the 2030 Agenda for Sustainable Development and the 17 Sustainable Development Goals (SDGs) at its core. The 2030 Agenda clearly recognizes that the rule of law and fair,

effective and humane justice systems, as well as health-oriented responses to drug use, are both enablers for and part of sustainable development.

Ghada Fathi

Ghada Fathi Waly is the Director-General/ Executive Director of the United Nations Office at Vienna (UNOV)/ United Nations Office on Drugs and Crime (UNODC) since 1 February 2020, following her appointment by Secretary-General António Guterres. She holds the rank of Under-Secretary-General of the United Nations. Ms. Waly's work experience includes 28 years in the field of poverty reduction and social protection. She served as Minister of Social Solidarity of Egypt from March 2014 until December 2019. She also served as the Coordinator of the Inter-Ministerial Committee for Social Justice and chaired the Executive Council of Arab Ministers of Social Affairs in the League of Arab States from 2014 to 2019. She was the Chairperson of Nasser Social Bank, a pro-poor developmental financial institution. She chaired the boards of the National Center for Social and Criminology Research, the National Fund for Drug and Addiction Control and the National Authority of Pensions and Social Insurance, which serves 25 million Egyptians.

Intelligence from Operation Weka II unveils Togo location of schoolgirl trafficked from Burkina Faso OUAGADOUGOU, Burkina Faso – Police cooperation via INTERPOL has enabled Togo police to release a teenage girl from sexual exploitation and reunite her with her family in Burkina Faso. The 17-year old schoolgirl went missing from her Ouagadougou home in January. She was identified as a potential trafficking victim during last month's Operation Weka II, an INTERPOL-led crackdown on the criminal groups behind human trafficking and migrant smuggling across 44 countries worldwide. After rescuing the kidnapped girl, Togo police brought her to the INTERPOL National Central Bureau (NCB) in Lomé where NCB officers arranged for her return to Burkina Faso. NCB Lomé officers accompany the girl from the police headquarters, which houses the Togo NCB , to her Burkina Faso flight on Friday 8 July. The 17-year old schoolgirl had gone missing several months earlier and was subsequently identified as a potential trafficking victim during INTERPOL's Operation Weka II. The girl was met by NCB Ouagadougou staff upon her arrival in Burkina Faso. NCB Ouagadougou staff accompany the rescued girl to meet her family upon arrival in Burkina Faso. Police cooperation via INTERPOL enabled Togo police to release the girl from sexual exploitation and reunite her with her mother in Burkina Faso Head of NCB Burkina Faso Commissaire Principal Daoud Traore also welcomed the rescued school girl back to her home country 1 / 8 Just a phone call away from freedom Secretly using one of the

kidnapper's mobile phones, the girl had called her parents who notified Burkina Faso authorities that their missing daughter had been kidnapped, and that she had called from a number in Togo.

15 suspects arrested in operation against human trafficking and child exploitation. ABIDJAN, Côte d'Ivoire – An INTERPOL-led operation targeting the criminal groups behind human trafficking and child exploitation across Benin, Burkina Faso, Côte d'Ivoire and Togo has seen 90 victims rescued and 15 suspected traffickers arrested. Of those rescued during Operation Priscas (5-12 December), 56 were underage victims of sexual exploitation and forced labour in gold mines, open-air markets and domestic settings. To ensure appropriate follow-up, social services and non-governmental organizations were identified and integrated into each country's operational plan. Victims were then taken into care for post-operation interviews and support. Operational highlights. In Côte d'Ivoire, authorities carried out several raids and vehicle checks on major routes. In a significant bust, one of those checks led to the identification of a group of 35 victims, including eight minors, who were accompanied by a known human trafficking suspect and his accomplice. Long suspected of running a business-like sexual exploitation ring, the pair had been wanted at national level for two years. Hoping to blend among the victims, they were caught when officers cross-checked their identity documents against INTERPOL's West African Police Information System (WAPIS). In Burkina Faso, thanks to

vehicle profiling, 10 minors were identified as they travelled to an illegal gold mine, where they had been promised work. The children, who did not have any identity documents on them, were taken into care and their 'employer' arrested. Investigations are ongoing.

More than 250 human traffickers and people smugglers behind bars after Pan American police operation. Operation Turquesa IV aimed to identify and dismantle criminal organizations exploiting the world's most vulnerable LYON, France - An INTERPOL operation targeting human trafficking and migrant smuggling across Latin America and the Caribbean has seen victims rescued, migrants detected and suspected perpetrators arrested in 32 countries. The fourth in INTERPOL's 'Turquesa' series of operations, the five-day (28 November – 2 December) operation saw Latin American investigators use INTERPOL capabilities to work with police forces on all continents to generate investigative leads and disrupt the global crime groups behind people trafficking and migrant smuggling. Frontline officers conducted controls at trafficking and smuggling hotspots identified ahead of operations, with particular emphasis on transit points such as airports, bus terminals and border crossings. Although results are still coming in, preliminary reporting points to the arrest of 268 individuals suspected of involvement in migrant smuggling, human trafficking, or associated crime such as document fraud and sexual offences. A total of 9,015 irregular migrants were detected, and 128 women and two men rescued from human trafficking. Most of the trafficked victims were from Colombia and Venezuela. Frontline officers conduct controls at suspected trafficking and smuggling hotspots in Belize. Bolivian authorities investigate suspected cases of sex trafficking where criminals are thought to have used fraud and coercion to recruit, transport, and force their victims to work as prostitutes in La Paz.

"Human trafficking and migrant smuggling are multi-billion euro criminal industries, bankrolling the world's most dangerous organized crime groups and violating the fundamental rights of victims in the process," said INTERPOL Secretary General Jürgen Stock. "The stories we hear of exploitation on global migrant trails in operations like Turquesa IV are heartbreaking, and law enforcement has a duty to safeguard the victims while bringing the perpetrators to justice," added Secretary General Stock. Sustainable, long-term impact. To share contemporary investigation and victim interview techniques, strengthen the region's ability to investigate cases of human trafficking and migrant smuggling, and support cooperation at the regional and international levels, Turquesa IV's action phase was preceded by training workshops. INTERPOL's National Central Bureau in Chile supported participating countries' operational and investigative needs throughout the week-long operation by hosting a dedicated coordination unit staffed by local and INTERPOL *experts on financial crime, human trafficking and migrant smuggling. A cross-sector, coordinated approach involving CARICOM IMPACS, UNODC, IOM and Europol enabled Operation Turquesa IV to combine collective strengths and exchange best practices for maximum results on the ground whilst also ensuring victims received appropriate care and protection throughout the judicial processes. Funded by GAC Global Affairs Canada, Operation Turquesa IV is the second operation of its kind to be coordinated with the support of INTERPOL's 'PROTEGER' Project which aims to strengthen law enforcement capacity in Latin America and the Caribbean to stem migrant smuggling, with special attention to gender considerations.*

Trafficking for forced labour. Victims of this widespread form of trafficking come primarily from developing countries. They are recruited and trafficked using deception and coercion and find themselves held in conditions of slavery in a variety of jobs. Victims can be engaged in agricultural, mining, fisheries or construction work, along with domestic servitude and other labour-intensive jobs. INTERPOL operations have rescued trafficked men, women and children from forced labour. This crime is not limited to a single region or demographic.

Trafficking in women for sexual exploitation. This prevalent form of trafficking affects every region in the world, either as a source, transit or destination country. Women and children from developing countries, and from vulnerable parts of society in developed countries, are lured by promises of decent employment into leaving their homes and travelling to what they consider will be a better life. Victims are often provided with false travel documents and an organized network is used to transport them to the destination country, where they find themselves forced into sexual exploitation and held in inhumane conditions and constant terror.

Children largely from the ethnic Dom community learn in a UNICEF-supported centre in Jordan, in 2019. With many of their families living in poverty, these children become especially vulnerable to negative coping mechanisms, like working on the street. Centres play a key role in identifying children who face challenges and helping them to enroll in formal and non-formal education.

Recent years have seen significant progress in the fight against child labour. The current COVID-19 pandemic, however, can potentially reverse the positive trends observed in several countries and further aggravate the problem in regions where child labour has been more resistant to policy and programme measures. The level of global economic integration and the current crisis are likely to have a large and possibly lasting

worldwide adverse socio-economic and financial impact. The pandemic is increasing economic insecurity causing disruptions in supply chains, falling commodity prices, in particular oil, and halting the manufacturing industry. The financial markets have been particularly affected, tightening liquidity conditions in many countries and creating unprecedented outflows of capital in many economies. This joint UNICEF and ILO briefing paper discusses the main channels through which the current pandemic can influence child labour, including fall in living standards; deteriorating employment opportunities; rise in informality; reduction in remittances and migration; contraction of trade and foreign direct investment; temporary school closures; health shocks; pressure on public budgets and international aid flows.

Economic hardship exacts a toll on millions of families worldwide – and in some places, it comes at the price of a child's safety. Roughly 160 million children were subjected to child labour at the beginning of 2020, with 9 million additional children at risk due to the impact of COVID-19. This accounts for nearly 1 in 10 children worldwide. Almost half of them are in hazardous work that directly endangers their health and moral development. Children may be driven into work for various reasons. Most often, child labour occurs when families face financial challenges or uncertainty – whether due to poverty,

sudden illness of a caregiver, or job loss of a primary wage earner. The consequences are staggering. Child labour can result in extreme bodily and mental harm, and even death. It can lead to slavery and sexual or economic exploitation. And in nearly every case, it cuts children off from schooling and health care, restricting their fundamental rights and threatening their futures. Migrant and refugee children – many of whom have been uprooted by conflict, disaster or poverty – also risk being forced into work and even trafficked, especially if they are migrating alone or taking irregular routes with their families. Trafficked children are often subjected to violence, abuse and other human rights violations. And some may be forced to break the law. For girls, the threat of sexual exploitation looms large, while boys may be exploited by armed forces or groups. Children on the move risk being forced into work or even trafficked – subjected to violence, abuse and other human rights violations.

From child marriage to human trafficking, 18-year-old UNICEF-Reporter Rifa uses a computer tablet to raise awareness of the dangers that girls face, in the Cox's Bazar refugee camp, in Bangladesh. Human traffickers now have a huge presence in cyberspace with digital platforms used to recruit, exploit, and control victims; reach out to potential clients; and hide criminal proceeds – taking advantage of the speed, cost-effectiveness and anonymity of the Internet.

While walking home from school in Yoro, Honduras, the 13-year-old girl in the middle was grabbed, thrown into a van, beaten, raped and released one hour later. Societal violence has a profound impact on a child's ability to remain in school, especially in neighbourhoods where criminal gangs can act with impunity, leading to executions, movement restrictions and death threats, according to UNICEF.

National Agency for the Prohibition of Trafficking in Persons (NAPTIP), yesterday, rescued five under-aged labourers and sealed a building under construction in Enugu. The construction site, a four-storey building is located at N0. 1 Dr. Alex Ekwueme Street, Independence Layout, Enugu. South East Zonal Commander of NAPTIP, Nneka Ajie, said the raid followed an intelligence gathered by the agency that some

under-aged children were being exploited by their 'principal.' "We got a tip-off that some children are being brought into the state for child and exploitative labour. We carried out surveillance and raided the location. "We succeeded in rescuing five minors between the ages of eight and 17 and 12 adults who were minors as at the time they were recruited and brought to the state four years ago," she said.

New research developed jointly by the International Labour Organization (ILO) and the Walk Free Foundation, in partnership with the International Organization for Migration (IOM), has revealed the true scale of modern slavery around the world. The data, released during the United Nations General Assembly, shows that more than 40 million people around the world were victims of modern slavery in 2016. The ILO have also released a companion estimate of child labour, which confirms that about 152 million children, aged between 5 and 17, were subject to child labour.

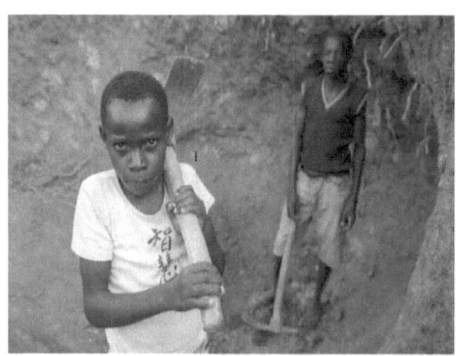

Child labour, forced labour, human trafficking and modern slavery are grievous issues of concern throughout the world. According to the African Union Ten Year Action Plan on Eradication of Child Labour, Forced Labour, Human Trafficking and Modern Slavery in Africa (2020-2030), in 2016, a fifth of African children (72 million) were in child labour. Nearly half of them were in hazardous work. The continent had both the largest number of child labourers and the highest proportion of children in child labour among the major world regions. The report stated that the number of victims of forced labour, human trafficking and modern slavery was also large: nearly 3 million adults and about half a million children were in forced labour; another 5.8 million people were in forced marriages. In general, women and girls are greatly affected by these forms of exploitation. Africa has worked relentlessly to fight these scourges, which typically afflict the most vulnerable populations on the continent. The scourges have long been targeted for eradication by a number of continental legal instruments and policy frameworks, notably the African Charter on Human and Peoples' Rights and the African Charter on the Rights and Welfare of the Child.

Irene Wanzila, 10, works breaking rocks with a hammer at the Kayole quarry in Nairobi, Kenya, Sept. 29, 2020, along with her younger brother, older sister and mother in Cape Town. The 5th Global Conference on the Elimination of Child Labor is taking place in Durban, South Africa. The latest figures given by the International Labor Organization show child labor has increased for the first time since they started measuring twenty years ago. Today there are 160 million children in child labor.

Vulnerable Nigerian Women Struggle on Italian Streets. Nigerian streetwalker on the main street in Castel Volturno plying her trade. Italian authorities say one out of every two sex worker on the roads of Italy are Nigerian. (Photo: Jamie Dettmer for VOA)

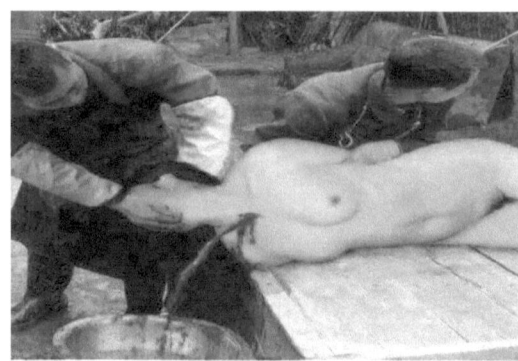

According to the Protocol to Prevent, Suppress and Punish Trafficking in Persons, especially Women and Children: "Exploitation shall include, at a minimum, ... the removal of organs". Trafficking in Persons for the Removal of Organs (TPRO) includes the removal of organs as an end purpose of trafficking. TPRO occurs across the globe and may be stepped up with the increase of transplant practices and poor regulation on these practices. For instance, the issue of forced removal of organs in the context of trafficking in persons and migrant smuggling in North-Eastern Africa gained renewed international attention in July 2016. The investigation revealed that Eritrean migrants, who had been kidnapped along the route to North Africa and who were unable to pay ransoms, were killed to remove their organs. The organs were then sold for around US$15,000.

References

https://www.un.org/en/chronicle/article/prevention-prosection-and-protection-human-trafficking

https://www.unodc.org/unodc/en/human-Trafficking/Human-Trafficking.html

United Nations Office on Drugs and Crime

shttps://www.britannica.com/stopic/human-trafficking

https://apps.who.int/iris/bitstream/handle/10665/77394/WHO_RHR_12.42_eng.pdf;sequence=1

https://www.unicef.org/protection/child-labour

https://www.ilo.org/global/topics/forced-labour/lang--en/index.htm

https://www.interpol.int/en/Crimes/Human-trafficking

About the Author

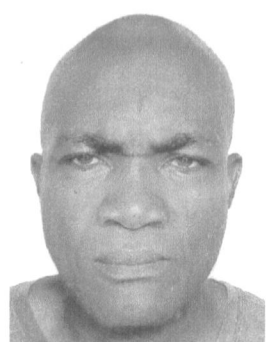

Bright Mills

Best selling author Bright Mills is a writer, an engineer and a historian from Nigeria. He has a degree in Information Technology. He is a creative writer and have written so many books in Fiction and non fiction. His books have received starred reviews weekly, library journal, and Book list. He promises to pull heart strings, offer a few laughs, and share tidbits of tantalizing history. His work has been praised by many.

www.ingramcontent.com/pod-product-compliance
Lightning Source LLC
LaVergne TN
LVHW041540070526
838199LV00046B/1754